seventeen

the boyfriend clinic

the final word on
FLIRTING, DATING, GUYS, and LOVE

by **MELANIE MANNARINO**
senior editor of **seventeen**

A PARACHUTE PRESS BOOK 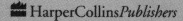 HarperCollins*Publishers*

Created and produced by
PARACHUTE PUBLISHING, L.L.C.
156 Fifth Avenue, Suite 302
New York, NY 10010

Published by
HarperCollins*Publishers*
1350 Avenue of the Americas
New York, NY 10019

For information write:
Editorial Manager, **seventeen**
850 Third Avenue
New York, NY 10022

Design by Bill Anton / Service Station
Cover photograph by Anna Palma
Printed in Baltimore, Maryland by John D. Lucas Printing

Library of Congress Cataloging-in-Publication Data

Mannarino, Melanie.
  The boyfriend clinic: the final word on flirting, dating, guys, and love /
  Melanie Mannarino.
    p.   cm. — (Seventeen)
  Summary: Offers advice to teenage girls with questions about how to get a
  boyfriend and what to do once you've got one.
  ISBN 0-06-447235-3 (pbk.)
  1. Teenage girls — Juvenile literature. 2. Dating (Social customs) — Juvenile
  literature. [1. Dating (Social customs)] I. Title. II. Series

  HQ798.M298 2000   00-26976
  646.7'7'08352—dc21   CIP
                                        AC

10 9 8 7 6 5 4 3 2 1

First Printing August 2000

Table of CONTENTS

ACKNOWLEDGMENTS

Many thanks to Andrea Chambers, Patrice Adcroft, and my editor, Eloise Flood. And thank you to Jamie, my husband, who proved that being my giggly, goofy self was the best way to get a guy.

Introduction

*I have liked this boy since the beginning of the new term.
I see him every day before school starts. I want to go on a date
with him, but I don't even know how to begin. What should
I do?*

NO, WE HAVEN'T BEEN READING YOUR DIARY. But we're
willing to bet that the letter above, from a **seventeen** reader, sounds
familiar to you.

Do you sometimes wonder just *when* you started crushing on
boys so hard, and how you'll ever be able to get them to crush
back? Things have changed a bit since you were a kid. Back then,
you and your girlfriends hung out with boys after school, tore up
the neighborhood in a pack on weekends, and went to each
other's birthday parties. The girls and the boys used to be one big
happy group, playing in Little League together and teasing the
rival teams.

But now everything's different. Behind every conversation or
good-natured teasing lies a strange new feeling. Suddenly, a
group trip to the movies is filled with expectations and anxieties.
Forget about the movie—you and your girlfriends have more
important things to think about. Like, will you be able to casually
snag a seat next to the boy you like? Will he offer to buy you
popcorn? What if he tries to slide into the seat next to your best

friend? And though these crowd dates are fun, you're starting to think it would be nice to spend some time with just one boy.

That's right, it's started. You're heading into the dating years.

Going from girl friend to *girlfriend* is exciting and nerve-wracking at the same time. There are so many factors involved, and developing a crush on the (seemingly) most perfect guy for you is only the beginning. Relationships can take work, whether you and your guy are in the beginning stages, wondering who should call whom first, or you're heavy into the dating phase, making out big-time as the credits roll, and wondering how far you should go.

Luckily, we've got you covered. This book will take you through all aspects of dating, from figuring out whether a crush on your best guy friend will result in love, to flirting with flair, to deciding what gift to buy your boyfriend to celebrate a three-month anniversary. You'll read letters from readers who have the same questions you do, quotes from teenage guys offering their opinions of the dating game, and tips from teenage girls who have been there, done that—and gone on to fall in love again. Plus, we'll give you realistic, foolproof solutions to every possible love problem you might have.

What more could you possibly need? (Besides a boyfriend, of course.)

chapter 1

You Like Him?

There's this really gorgeous guy who rides my bus every morning. I don't know him, I've never even spoken to him—but I am totally in love! I can't stop thinking about him! What is wrong with me?

IT IS SO EASY TO DEVELOP A CRUSH ON A GUY, and sometimes it can feel like it happened overnight. But no matter how fast it happens, or how often you catch yourself daydreaming about him in social studies, there is *nothing* wrong with you.

Maybe he first caught your eye when he rushed in to homeroom seconds before the bell rang. Then you realized that his locker was three down from yours, and when you jammed your coat in your locker door one day, he laughed *with* you—not at you—as he helped you get it unstuck. Now you find yourself looking for him in the hallways, and you made it your business to find out that he has third-period lunch.

It can happen just like that. You get caught off guard by a crush, and before you know it, thinking about him has turned into your full-time hobby. In other words: You're sweating him bad.

But while it's easy to crush on a guy you barely know, it is really hard to see whether this crush might develop into something deeper—that is, until you at least know his middle name. That's why, when you have a crush, you need to collect as much information as possible about that adorable guy you're in like with.

Besides getting the scoop on whether you and he have anything in common, it also makes sense to figure out whether he's romantically available and in a position to like you back. If you're crushing on your big sister's boyfriend, for example, you have to realize that a relationship will never work.

HERE ARE A FEW CLUES TO HELP YOU DECIDE IF HE'S RIGHT FOR YOU:

Do you like him for *him*? It's easy to fall for the stereotypical bad boy (or jock, or intellectual), but if you are falling in love with an image you need to go deeper. What is it you like about him? That he hangs with the mysterious grunge-heads at the back of the school, scrawling graffiti on brick walls? Or have you learned that behind his tough exterior, he's a vegetarian like you and is also interested in Native American history?

If you are simply dazzled by what he represents, then there is no future. But if you appreciate all that he is, then this relationship has a solid chance.

Do you have similar interests? Yes, opposites most definitely attract, but if you and he have no interest in each other's likes and dislikes, it'll be a mighty boring match. This is why it's logical that you'd fall for your co-chair on the community service committee, your co-worker at Burger Barn, or your bandmate. There's no pressure to be *exactly* alike, but at least make sure his *Star Wars* babble doesn't put you to sleep.

Is he a nice guy? He doesn't have to spend his free time escorting old ladies across the street, but it would be a good sign if he treats you, his friends, and his classmates with respect. It's cool if you find his lunchtime rants on the history class rent-a-sub amusing; it's scary if you overlook his nasty habit of giving the younger boys wedgies during gym class.

Is there a chance you'll get together? Don't pine away for the Brazilian boy you met on a camping weekend. Letters and e-mails can sustain a friendship, but if his next planned trip to the States is not until next year, you might want to start dating other boys. Long-distance relationships are really hard to keep going. Likewise, it's always fun to have a crush on a celebrity, but it shouldn't hold you back from finding a date to the homecoming dance. Realistically, what are the chances of even *meeting* Freddie Prinze, Jr.—let alone scoring a date with him?

HOTTIE ALERT

While you may sometimes feel as if you'll never meet *anyone*, you only need to look around to see that every day you have dozens of opportunities to meet boys. In fact, in your whole life, you'll probably never have as many cutie encounters as you do right now.

That doesn't mean you *have* to have a crush on a guy. Between volleyball practice, science club, and your volunteer work at the senior citizens' center, you've got plenty going on right now. It's just that it's so easy to fall in like when you're surrounded by lots of potential crushes. Check out the number of hotties you might encounter on a given school day:

1 Wake up, get dressed, walk/hop on the bus to school. *Traveling hottie alert.*

2 Get to school, hit your locker, and then head to homeroom. *Hallway hottie alert.* (Those of you who attend all-girl schools can skip down to No. 4.)

3 Go to class. *Classroom hottie alert.* Multiply by the number of classes in the day. Score an extra *hottie alert* if you have gym class with mixed grades.

4 Lunch in the cafeteria/outside the building/at the local sandwich shop. *Lunchtime hottie alert.*

5 School ends, and you either:

- **a** Stay after for sports or club. *After-school hottie alert.*
- **b** Walk/take the bus home. *Another traveling hottie alert.*
- **c** Hang out at the local diner/ice cream stand/library. *Hangout hottie alert.*

6 Put in a few hours at your part-time job. *Worktime hottie alert.*

7 Eat dinner at home, go to bed, and rest your eyes. You've seen enough cuties for one day!

As you can see, even girls who go to all-girl schools have plenty of opportunities to meet boys, each and every day.

OBJECTS OF YOUR AFFECTION

When you're surrounded by guys all day long, it's natural to get starry-eyed about those closest to you. But every so often an iffy boy choice pops up.

How can you tell if you've made a not-so-great decision? Hint: While your heart is saying "Heck, yes!" your mind is screeching "What are you thinking?" Will a relationship with your mom's ex-boyfriend work out? The answer to that is a loud NO. Read on to see which other guys are sure to be a match made in heaven—or elsewhere.

THE OLDER GUY

There is this boy that I really like, and he likes me. We take the bus together, and he shows signs of being into me. There's one problem. He is a senior in high school, and I'm in ninth grade. Would it be wrong to start a relationship?

Dating an older guy is a thrill, and you know what they say about girls being light-years ahead of boys their own age, maturity-wise. However, with inclusion into a hip, older crowd comes

- The possibility of his friends resenting you
- Your friends wanting to tag along
- Your parents worrying about his intentions
- You having a way earlier curfew than he does

Can it work? Absolutely—as long as you and he acknowledge the difference your age makes.

THE YOUNGER GUY

I am sixteen, and I have a huge crush on this guy who's fourteen. He doesn't act or look like an average fourteen-year-old. I manage his sports team, and am around him hours at a time. What should I do?

Nothing makes a statement like dating a younger guy. It means you don't care what people think, and it says that you like this boy a whole lot—enough to withstand teasing from your friends and admiring stares from his. If you can take the heat, go for it.

YOUR BEST FRIEND'S BROTHER

My question is about dating my friend's brother. She has a really hot brother. I don't want to jeopardize our friendship, but I don't think she knows I like him as much as I do.

The thing about your best friend is, she knows you're there when she needs you (and vice versa). So if you're calling her house and she's not quite sure who you called to speak to, there are bound to be problems. It's even harder if she doesn't have a boyfriend of her own. How can she possibly learn from your French-kissing experiences when you're learning from her brother?

Think about this one long and hard, because your bud-since-kindergarten may make you choose which relationship to lose.

YOUR BROTHER'S BEST FRIEND

My older brother's best friend has always been nice to me, and lately he asks my brother things like "Does your sister have a boyfriend?" One day, when he was leaving our house, he walked into my room to say good-bye and added, "I love you." Wow! I like him a lot, but he's my brother's best friend. I'm confused.

It can work—we're not saying it can't. If your brother supports this get-together, then go for it. He'd never steer his little sister wrong. But there are pitfalls. For instance, if you break up, the guy probably isn't going to stop hanging with your brother—and you might feel uncomfortable seeing him all the time.

More important, it might get a tad sticky when your honey and your brother are hanging out and your honey starts to recall a make-out anecdote. Your brother probably doesn't want to hear about your smooching style.

In the end, you should be guided by what your brother wants. After all, he was friends with his buddy well before you two started making goo-goo eyes at each other.

THE BOY WITH A GIRLFRIEND

There's this guy I like a lot, but he has a g-friend. I call him every day, and we have good convos. I don't want to break him and his girlfriend up, but I like him, and I think he might like me too. What do I do?

We won't lie: It's tempting. It's *such* an ego-boost to capture the heart of a guy who's supposedly already taken. But your ego will take a real beating as vicious rumors circulate about your uncaring attitude and his cheating heart.

Ultimately, you need to see him for what he really is—a guy who isn't ready for a serious relationship with *any* girl, and one who isn't true to his word. And how scary is it to be involved with someone you can't trust? Very.

YOUR BEST BOY FRIEND

I think I am in love with my best guy friend. We get along excellently, and we have everything in common. I am so confused—should I tell him how I feel and take a chance of ending the friendship?

Entire television shows are based on situations like this. You and he have been friends forever, telling each other your deepest secrets, offering advice on crushes...when suddenly you realize that your perfect match may be sitting right next to you.

Sealing this new phase in your relationship with a kiss is a risk—you might just break up one day, leaving each of you without a best bud. But you *can* make this match work. The key is to keep things honest and open. And you should definitely have a heart-to-heart discussion about whether you'll feel comfortable going back to friendship if the romance doesn't work out.

OFF-LIMIT LOVE INTERESTS

There are few absolutes when it comes to dating. However, we can think of a few popular crush objects with whom a passionate relationship will NEVER work.

THE YOUNG MALE TEACHER

Yes, it was so exciting when he danced with you at the Spring Fling. And you felt pretty cool when your friends brought it up jealously for weeks afterward. But he was a *chaperone*—not a fellow partyer. There is no way a relationship between you and a teacher will work out. So quit daydreaming and finish *Catcher in the Rye* already.

THE FATHER OF THE KIDS YOU BABY-SIT FOR

This movie-of-the-week's already been written, girls. Yes, he offers to drive you home while she puts the kids to bed, and he tells you the family couldn't survive without you. And maybe he even compliments you on your new sweater set. But he is a *married man*. Let's take apart that phrase: he's *married*, meaning off limits to you and every other female, and he's a *man*, whereas you are still a teenage girl.

That about says it, huh?

Whether you've got a list of ten boys you're dying to kiss or you like one guy in particular, it makes total sense to step back and consider the love match. Then, once you've determined that the stars are properly aligned, go for it. How? You've got to ROCK HIS WORLD! Read on....

chapter 2

Rock His World

I don't want to start my freshman year at school without a boyfriend. How can I get guys to notice me and ask me out?

NOT QUITE SURE HOW TO GET A GUY'S ATTENTION?

Well, you could sneeze really loudly in the library. Or you could trip over your long skirt by his locker.

But after you land flat on your face at the feet of your crush, don't assume that he'll lift you into his arms for a passionate kiss. It doesn't happen like that. Most likely he'll

a Give you a funny look and then walk away.

b Ask if you're okay and help you collect your scattered belongings

Obviously, choice b) is preferred. But in either case, that unexpected, sexy smooch will most likely remain just a dream. So how do you get a guy to think, "Man, I've got to ask her out"? Prepare to be amazed, because it really is simple. In fact, there are only two things you need to do to get noticed—the right way:

1 BE CONFIDENT. Here's a known fact: You are your own worst critic. Haven't you ever come to school in a cranky mood because your hair is misbehaving? And then been shocked when your friends tell you how great you look? Take it from us: Nobody but you fixates on the pimple on your nose or your snorting laugh. So make like the rest of the world and ignore these supposed flaws. Because nothing is sexier than self-confidence.

CONFIDENCE CHECKLIST

Test your own sense of self by **CHECKING OFF** the choice you'd make:

a) You walk into a room full of strangers with your head held high and a smile on your face.
b) You hurry, head down, to a chair closest to the door.

a) You raise your hand and ask your social studies teacher to repeat the homework directions.
b) You keep silent, feeling dumb for not understanding them the first time.

a) You refuse to go to school the day a large, red eruption occurs on your forehead.
b) You apply a little cover-up and the attitude that it's probably not as bad as you think.

a) You clear your throat and continue singing when your voice cracks during an "Ave Maria" solo.
b) You blush furiously, stutter an apology, and run out of the room.

a) You wear shapeless, bulky clothing to disguise your hideously scrawny/humongous figure.
b) You wear outfits that emphasize your favorite part of your body.

We don't need to tell you which choices represent sassy self-confidence. So if you find yourself identifying with three or more of the less self-assured actions, do yourself a favor and reread what we have to say about confidence.

2 BE YOURSELF. There are plenty of ways to catch the interest of a guy without faking a look, an attitude, or a hobby. Why pretend that you're an avid sports fan if in fact you can't tell a touchdown from a slam dunk? Instead, raise your hand in Spanish class and dazzle him by rattling off a sentence in the past tense. The only way you can truly shine is by letting others get to know the real you—whether you're a country music fan, a home-work perfectionist, a party girl—or any combination of the above.

YOU think/THEY think

Think you've got a major personality imperfection that's stopping you from scoring socially? **We've read thousands of letters from girls who complain about the "problems" listed below. But check out this chart to learn how others read your moves.**

	You think:	Other girls see:	He'll see:
Shy	No one could possibly be interested in what you have to say.	A girl who is comfortable with silences and doesn't need to babble to fill the air.	A mysterious girl who must have much on her mind — and he's dying to know what it is.
Loud	Your inner volume control must be broken, because you always laugh and speak way louder than you planned.	Someone who's as bold as they wish they were.	At last, a girl who isn't afraid to have fun and show it.
A Jock	You're always being treated like one of the guys, so there's no way a boy would like you.	You are so lucky—you have actual conversations with boys!	Someone who's great to talk to *and* who can beat him at one-on-one; all that's left to do is kiss you!

STALKING HIM
AND OTHER BAD MOVES

Now that you're empowered and confident and totally real, you're ready to be a woman of action. Why wait for him to approach you when you can make the first move? Many guys actually like bold girls, and showing him you like him is way more effective than repeating to yourself "Please let him like me." Yet keep in mind that hunting him down like he's Bambi during deer season isn't going to make him fall in love.

Check out the following situations, paying particular attention to the ones that sound all too familiar. Then read the kinder, gentler strategies we suggest. And remember:

THIS ISN'T WAR—*It's Love.*

If you often...snag his pen, baseball cap, or anything else while he's not looking, just to have a piece of him for your own...

Why not try...easing up on the kleptomania and asking him to sign your yearbook, lend you a pen, or rip a blank page out of his spiral so you can take notes in math.

If you often...talk friends or siblings into driving past his house so you can catch a glimpse of him through a window...

Why not try...convincing your older sister to drive past his house one weekday morning, so you can catch him walking to school and conveniently offer him a ride.

If you often…call his house, and then clam up totally when he picks up the phone and says "Hello? Is anyone there? Who is this?"

Why not try…thinking of a good reason to call, and then actually speaking to him. Reasonable excuses include:

a Asking him a question about an activity you're both involved in. For example, "Do you know how we're supposed to get to the debate on Saturday?"

b Getting a homework assignment. For example, "I sit behind you in biology; do you know which chapters are covered on tomorrow's quiz?"

c Something even more creative, like "I hear you're a great artist, and I was wondering: would you help me design campaign posters for the junior class elections?"

If you often…talk really loudly about fun and exciting things going on in your life whenever he's near, just to let him know how cool and interesting you are…

Why not try…being yourself around him. By all means, if you are naturally bubbly, keep up the high-volume chatter. But if you were practicing a notice-me move, let your actions speak loudly instead. Boys don't live in caves—he's probably already heard about your wacky adventure on the school roof, or seen your incredible performance as Abigail in the school production of *The Crucible*. You *are* cool—you don't need to explain why.

SEVENTEEN SIGNS HE LIKES YOU

Q *There is one question I keep asking people, but nobody ever gives me enough info: How can you tell if a guy likes you? What are the signs?*

A Though the inner thoughts of teenage boys are often hard to read, there are certain clues that provide insight into his emotions. Here are some of the most reliable ones:

1 He lends you his favorite hat.

2 He "just happens" to show up at the bowling alley where you work—even though it's across town, there's a raging blizzard, and the Mommy and Me Bowling Classic is in full swing.

3 He cracks a joke in class, then whips his head in your direction to gauge your reaction.

4 He awkwardly compliments you. ("Hey, Jessica— I like your socks.")

5 He pulls a groin muscle in P.E., yet insists on playing volleyball on your team until the bell rings.

6 He teases you mercilessly by waving dead-frog innards in your face, then looks shocked and hurt when you turn green and shove him away.

7 He starts befriending all of your friends.

8 He stares at you in the halls, then drops to his knees to tie his shoe when you catch him.

9 He starts showing up at choir practice, drama rehearsal, and community service club meetings—all of your usual hangouts.

10 He starts riding your bus home, even though he lives a block away from school.

11 He play-tackles you to the ground during a fire drill.

12 He questions you endlessly about homework, your art project, your locker location, your favorite sitcom....

13 He makes like a mute when you talk to him—even if you're just saying "Excuse me" on the way to your desk.

14 He slants his paper your way during a pop quiz on *To Kill a Mockingbird*—which you just confessed you haven't read.

15 He calls you at home, then makes up a lame reason ("Um, did you call me? My mom said some girl named Megan called—I thought it was you.")

16 He picks you first for his War of the Classes relay team, knowing perfectly well you can't run and pass a baton at the same time.

17 He actually asks you out. On a date.

The DEAL

Here's what it comes down to:

Almost all guys are looking for the same qualities in a girlfriend. AND, BABY, YOU'VE GOT THEM. Take a peek at the following list of traits that make up the perfect girlfriend.

- She knows what she's good at—whether it's swing dancing or mathematical formulas—and doesn't hide it.

- She acts easygoing and natural—even around the cutest guy on the soccer field.

- She doesn't try too hard to get a guy's attention, but she does follow her instincts.

- She knows that the best way to get a guy to notice her is to treat him as if he were a potential best friend.

- She's savvy enough to catch on when he starts showing signs that he's interested in her.

See? It's really not so hard! All you need is some confidence in yourself—and you'll be the girl this list describes.

Now—once he does notice you, you've got to engage him in some captivating conversation. Not sure how to get started? Turn to the next chapter for surefire FLIRTING advice.

Make Your Move

I really like this guy, and I want to go out with him. But I am way too nervous to talk to him. We've talked before, with friends, but never one-on-one. How do I show him my great personality?

YOU'VE STARED LONGINGLY AT HIM. He's gazed adoringly at you. So how do you keep this momentum going?

Take a deep breath, relax, and *talk* to him. Oh, and before some of you skip ahead to the next chapter, let us remind you that passing back the weekly math exam while mumbling "Here you go" doesn't count. Don't get us wrong—it's a start. But flirting is like a really good TV movie: If it doesn't hook you in the first few minutes, the odds increase that you'll flip the channel. You're going to have to get his attention at the start.

Now tune in as we review move-making strategies.

FLIRT LIKE YOU MEAN IT

Here's the best flirting tip you'll ever get: Open your mouth and talk to a guy. As your charming, witty remarks make their way to his brain, he'll respond with clever retorts of his own, and before you know it your friends will be impressed by your flirting expertise. If it sounds simple, that's because it is.

That said, sometimes it's hard to get started, especially when your stomach is churning like Laura Ingalls Wilder making butter. Below are a few standard flirty tactics to inspire you.

THE SHOW-OFF FLIRT

Mission: To show this cutie that if he sticks with you, he'll learn a thing or two.

Situation: There you are, typing away in the media center, when he slides into the seat next to you. As he struggles to locate the power switch on the computer, you slyly look over at him and say, "Need any help? I know how tricky it can be turning on a PC."

His response: Most likely, he'll scrunch his eyebrows and explain that his computer at home is *much* different.

Continue this conversation: Once you've leaned over to turn on his monitor, ask him what he's working on. Suggest a study break in an hour—when you can chat him up a little more.

THE EYE-CONTACT FLIRT

Mission: To boldly get his attention, and use body language to initiate a conversation.

Situation: You're walking through the mall, swinging your shopping bags when you spot him—the hottest stranger you've ever seen. You stop, pause, and rewind, giving him a double take.

His response: He notes your double take, and takes the opportunity to toss his pretzel wrapper at the trash bin nearest you. As the wrapper hits the pail, he looks up and says "Hey."

Continue this conversation: This is where details are crucial. If he's carrying a bag from Abercrombie & Fitch, ask if they're having a big sale. Or ask if he knows where you can find the bookstore. (*He* doesn't know you hang out there all the time!) If all else fails, tell him his pretzel made you hungry, and ask him to point you in the direction of the food court. No matter how you approach him, be sure to keep the conversation going with more questions, like where he's from, what he's shopping for, whether he's heard the latest Korn CD, and so on.

THE "HEY, ME TOO" FLIRT

Mission: To take advantage of common interests, which are the building blocks for any solid relationship.

Situation: You're spending a solitary Saturday at the county museum, researching your town's history for a school project. As you step back to view a wall-size mural of the town at the turn of the century, you bump into the new guy from class. "Hi," you say, surprised. "I guess you're working on Mr. Rossi's project, too."

His response: "You guessed it," he might reply. "How weird is it that people used to mine for gold in this town?"

Continue this conversation: Ding, ding, ding! Common ground! Suggest teaming up to do your research together, and arrange to meet tomorrow to work on the report some more. That way you'll have time to find out what else you may have in common.

THE FLATTERY FLIRT

Mission: To show your hopeful honey that you like what you see.

Situation: You spot the guy you like attempting a way challenging task: He's the only ninth grader going out for varsity football. After he gets crushed during practice (literally), tell him how great he was out on the field.

His response: He knows you're lying, but he'll say "Hey, thanks" anyway. Because what you're really doing is telling him that you recognize his efforts.

Continue this conversation: Ask him if he's up for a quick plate of French fries with cheese at the diner. He needs to bulk up if he intends to lead the junior varsity team to victory this season. Over fries, you can rely on the staples of any getting-to-know-you convo: music, movies, television.

THE "I HATE YOU/I LOVE YOU" FLIRT

Mission: To morph your passionate argument into another kind of passion.

Situation: Your crush just happens to be the supercute guy who's running against you for student council president. You're right in the middle of a heated debate over the merits of school uniforms— he thinks they're a good idea; you totally disagree. Spotting a flaw in his argument, you snap out a sassy comeback.

His response: No matter what he says, if he loses his train of thought every time you look him in the eye, he's probably hooked.

Continue this conversation: Grab him in the hall after class and ask if he wants to convince you to see his side at lunch over a slice-n-soda at Joey's Pizza. Even if you both agree to disagree, you can move on to topics you might see eye to eye on—like which movie you both really want to catch this weekend.

THE FULL-ON FLIRT

Mission: To eliminate any confusion whatsoever, and let him know that you are flirting with him.

Situation: You're hobbling to class on your new crutches after twisting your ankle in kickline practice. You're shocked when that upperclassman you've always stared at from afar comes up and offers to carry your bookbag. Thinking fast, you drawl, "If I'd known you'd offer to help, I'd have twisted my ankle months ago."

His response: Inspired by your bold declaration, he'll likely respond in kind: "I'm here to help—use me!"

Continue this conversation: If he does offer unlimited assistance, tell him you wouldn't mind help getting home from school, if he's got time later.

All of these flirting techniques should end in the same way—with the two of you discussing everything from your favorite color to your least favorite pizza topping. And even if love lights don't go off in both your heads, you're still getting to know a person who's probably pretty cool and worth being friends with.

PHONE 411: A CHEAT SHEET FOR SMOOTH CONVERSATIONS

Here's what's nice about a guy asking for your number: You can just sit back and wait for him to call you.

Here's what's nice about calling him yourself: You don't have to sit around nervously waiting for the phone to ring.

No matter who punches the buttons, certain calling skills can really make a phone call flow. The who, what, when, where, why, and how of phone conversations are the essential tools you need to really connect with a cutie over the phone.

Who should you call? Do call a guy if you never get the chance to talk to him in person, and you really want to speak with him. Don't call a boy for your shy best friend (her crush may have more fun talking with *you*—which could create an awkward love triangle). Don't call a boy who has a girlfriend already.

What should you say? Say whatever is on your mind. This is your chance to talk to him without getting lost in his chocolate-brown eyes or his incredible pectorals. He doesn't know you're sitting there with cream hair remover on your upper lip, he can't tell that your ears are burning bright red, and he won't notice if you're pacing back and forth so hard that you're in danger of wearing track marks in your bedroom rug. You've got his attention, without any visual distractions.

When do you call? Use your best judgment here. If you know he works at the gas station until 7:30 every night, don't call his house at 7:45—he'll probably be eating dinner. In fact, even if you don't know anything about his extracurricular schedule, steer clear of dinnertime hours. If your mom gets annoyed when phone calls interrupt the family meal, his parents might feel the same way. And wouldn't you hate to be the cause of a family argument? A general rule of thumb is to call before 6 P.M., or between 8 and 10 P.M. After you've spoken on the phone once, you two can make a mutual plan for the next phone conversation.

Where should you call from? Don't grab a stool at the breakfast nook and try to have a private conversation with your crush while your little sister and her friends are making Popsicle-stick doll furniture at the kitchen table. Try to get as much privacy as you can, without resorting to locking yourself in the bathroom (somebody is bound to need it!). The more peaceful your calling environment, the calmer you'll feel while talking with him.

Why are you calling, again? Have a reason. Even if it's just to ask for his address, because you're thinking about throwing a party and you want to send him an invitation. Calling a boy without having anything to say is like telling a friend you have a knock-knock joke, and then asking her to start it. Think about it.

How can you tell if he's into the conversation? That's a tough one. Some boys resort to yes-or-no answers no matter who they're speaking with. Others use single-word sentences as a subtle hint that they'd rather be clipping their toenails. Without obsessing over it, go with your gut. If he takes thirty seconds to respond to a simple question like "Do we have a quiz in English tomorrow?" he's just clued you in to where this little chat ranks on his Important Activities scale. (Low.) But if he laughs at things you say and responds to your question with some of his own, he's probably glad you called.

TELEPHONE DOS AND DON'TS

DO remind him who you are—immediately. ("Hi, this is Maria. I sit in front of you in homeroom.")

DON'T play scary stalker guessing games. ("You don't know me, but I watch you at lacrosse practice every afternoon. How's that scrape on your shin healing?")

DO leave a message (make sure you include your name and number!) if you get the answering machine. Then he has to call you back.

DON'T call his house and hang up. In the age of Caller ID, *69, and other technological tracking devices, it's a move that can backfire.

DO remain calm if your mom picks up the phone while you're on. Resist the impulse to nervously shriek, "Mom! Hang up! I'm on the *phone!*"

DON'T call him to ask if he called you earlier. You know he didn't, and so does he.

THE THRILLS
OF TECHNOLOGY

Lucky you! Thanks to the Internet, you're able to meet guys who live across the country and around the world—from the safety and comfort of your own home.

Just remember, the Internet is cool and useful, but there are some safety precautions you should take when in chat rooms or e-mailing strangers. For example, you just met "plaidboy23" in a Depeche Mode chat room. He claims to be a big fan of '80s New Wave music and a junior at a high school on the East Coast. The problem is, how can you know that any of it is true? Maybe he's some thirty-seven-year-old sicko who thinks you are the woman of his dreams. Eww, right?

If you're online, you can never be totally sure to whom you are revealing your secret wishes and desires, not to mention your phone number or address. The Internet rocks, but keep it light, keep it casual, and most important, keep your personal info to yourself.

Now, let's say you've been carrying on a six-month-long e-mail friendship with a boy, and the two of you are dying to meet each other. We've got to tell you, it's risky. But you can make it less so.

How can you play it safe while playing it cool? Arrange to meet him at a public place—like the diner downtown—and tell him your parents will be driving you there. Once you're there and have met him, ask your parents to take a booth near the door. Then usher your guy to a table far enough away from your parents so you can have a private conversation, but close enough so that he can't kidnap you. Then see if the sparks fly between the two of you in person as fast as they do when you're flirting online.

THE SOUND OF SILENCE

Every time I call a boy, I find that I have nothing interesting to say, and then we both end up saying nothing. What can I talk about to keep the conversation going?

There you are, having an amazing phone conversation with the cute sophomore whose name you doodle in your notebook, when talk slows to a halt. And you don't know what to do. In an attempt to fill the dead air, you get even more tongue-tied. You've gone from feeling excited and spunky to feeling self-conscious and completely insecure about this new relationship. Panic sets in, and he, equally alarmed by the lengthy pause (trust us), clears his throat and says he guesses he'll see you in school tomorrow. You hang up, totally bummed and confused. How did that happen?

Before you conclude that you're the only twosome that has ever fallen victim to abrupt silences, let us assure you that these pauses are very common, whether they occur in person, over the phone, or even in an instant-messaged cyber chat. The key is to be prepared for conversational lulls. Silences can occur for a number of reasons, but rarely is there a reason to get freaked out by them. Consider these situations:

1 YOU'VE EXHAUSTED A TOPIC

Tactic: Treat the moment of silence like the end of a chapter in a book (read: a necessary break). Then, after a beat or two, go on to another subject.

Example:

> He: "Well, if you really want to get into the typing class, maybe you should speak to the teacher after school."
> You: "Yeah, I guess you're right."
> *pause*
> You: "So, who did you say was coming over Friday night?"

2 ONE OF YOU HAS SAID SOMETHING INCREDIBLY STUPID

Tactic: If you goofed, acknowledge it with genuine remorse. If he stuck his foot in his mouth, accept his apology and move on.

Example:

> He: "The coffee shop guy treated me like I was a retard!"
> You: "My sister is mentally challenged, you know."
> *pause*
> He: "Oh, I'm sorry. I didn't know."
> You: "Well, she is." (Switch tone to lighthearted.) "And I've got to tell you: She knows the difference between a latte and an espresso, silly! How could you get confused?"

3

ONE OF YOU HAS SAID SOMETHING SIGNIFICANT

Tactic: Take advantage of the silence to formulate an equally serious response. Then respond directly. If this only sparks another silence, follow it up with a clever subject-switch.

Example:

> He: "I really like you—as more than a friend."
> *pause*
> You: "I really like you a lot, too, but right now I am more interested in keeping you as a friend than starting a boyfriend-girlfriend relationship."
> *pause*
> You: "Speaking of girlfriends and boyfriends, do you think someone could tell Rich and Jan to keep their tongues in their own mouths during homeroom?"

4

YOU SPACED OUT, AND HE'S WAITING FOR YOU TO ANSWER HIS QUESTION (OR VICE VERSA).

Tactic: Come clean and explain why you spaced. Then ask him to repeat the question.

Example:

> *pause*
> He: "Hello? Did you hear what I said?
> You: "Oh—yeah. Sorry. My cat was just scaling the screen door. What did you ask me again?"

These guys survived some awkward moments.

"I called a girl I hadn't spoken to in four years with the intention of asking her out. She didn't remember who I was. But I reminded her—and when I finally did ask her out, she said yes."
—Drew

"I asked this girl to a dance, and she said no. I felt like an idiot. But still, you've gotta ask."
—Patrick

"I was trying to talk with a girl, and throughout our conversation my friends kept screaming that I had a crush on her."
—Vinny

TEN TIP-OF-YOUR-TONGUE TOPICS OF CONVERSATION

1 Talk about kids you both know in school. But don't put anyone down—it'll make you look mean, and you might be ragging on one of his friends.

2 Tell him about your family. If you're steaming from a fight with your older brother, ask your crush how he'd handle the situation.

3 Everyone has something to say about movies, music, or television. If you've seen the same flick, discuss your reactions to it. If he hasn't yet tuned in to your favorite sitcom, explain why it's so great.

4 Talk about class assignments. Even if he doesn't have the same English teacher, he might have already read *Fahrenheit 451* in class.

5 Discuss a topic that affects you both, like the driving age in your state, the movie ratings for kids under seventeen, or the huge number of your classmates who smoke cigarettes.

6 Do you have a pet? Want one? He's sure to have a pet story of his own, even if it's just about his allergic reactions to his grandparents' dog.

7 Are you baby-sitting, or working part-time at the yogurt shop? Tell a funny/interesting/crazy story from work. He may respond with one of his own.

8 Tell him about your extracurricular activities, like sports or clubs. Are you excited to have your artwork displayed at the local public library? Let him know.

9 Share your opinion on UFOs, and ask him what he thinks.

10 Find out what his plans are for the weekend. Is he going to the basketball game at the high school on Friday? Maybe you'll see him there.

You've crushed and you've flirted. You've called him (or he's called you), you've gotten to know him a little better, and you've analyzed every last bit of his behavior with all of your girlfriends. It sounds like the next step is getting together.

The question is: **WHAT ARE YOU GOING TO DO ABOUT IT?** For starters, you can turn to the next chapter. We'll weigh the pros and cons of waiting for him to ask, getting your friends to play Cupid, or just sucking it up and asking him out yourself. (**DON'T STRESS**—it's not as scary as you think!)

chapter 4

The Dating Game

I have a crush at school. We've talked and flirted a few times, and I've noticed him staring at me. I think he likes me. But now I don't know what to do next.

Up to this point, you've been the one in control of your romantic destiny. You've chosen your crushes, you've flirted with anyone you liked, and you've gotten countless guys to notice you. But now you have a few signs that the boy you like actually likes you back. **SO HOW DO YOU GET A DATE?**

Well, what about asking him out?

Does that sound even more frightening than the latest *Scream* sequel? If it's too much for you, you have two other options: You can rely on him to do the asking, or you can get your friends to play go-between. Although asking him out yourself seems like the scariest approach, in reality each option has its own benefits, drawbacks, and anxiety levels.

Make him do all the work	Get a little help from your friends	Do it yourself
Pro You can wait for him to approach you and still be your cool, casual self— on the outside, at least.	If *your* friends talk to *his* friends, neither of you risks embarrassment or rejection. Whew.	You can plan to ask him on a low-humidity, good-hair day when you haven't had a garlic bagel for lunch.
Con You are at the mercy of both his courage and his personal timetable.	Somewhere along the line some information could get dropped or distorted.	You are exposing yourself and your feelings, with the possibility of flat-out rejection.
Anxiety Level Your only fear is that you'll both graduate from college before he gets up the nerve to ask you out.	You have to have faith in the reliability of the messengers for this to work.	This is the scariest move. But even if he says no, you'll feel proud you had the nerve to ask him out.

(Anxiety level from 1 to 10, where 1 = cool as a well-chilled cucumber and 10 = sweating like you just ate a bowl of five-alarm chili.)

(IF HE DOES ALL THE WORK)

So let's say he asks you out. Low pressure for you, high pressure for him. How can you accept without losing your cool (for example, squealing "Yesyesyes!" in the middle of the main lobby at school), yet still let him know you're totally psyched?

It's easy. No matter where he asks, no matter how many people are around or how he says it, just take a minute to enjoy this big event, breathe deeply, smile, and say, "Sure." That's all there is to it. And then, once you're in the comfort of your own home, feel free to do a goofy little "I've got a date" dance. You deserve it, you guy magnet.

IF YOUR FRIENDS DO ALL THE WORK

Okay. Your friends have talked to his friends, confirming that if he asked you out, you would *definitely* say yes. From now on, the two of you are on your own—and if you can't handle that, you may want to rethink this whole dating thing.

However, just because the time has come for him to ask and you to reply, it doesn't mean that once the deal is made, you can't bring the gang along on a first date. As we discuss over the next couple of pages, a date can be many things, including the ever-comfortable group get-together.

IF YOU DO ALL THE WORK

If you decide to ask him out (and why not?), you need a plan. To make planning a little easier, we've suggested a few common "date" ideas and given you dialogue.

You'll notice that only one of these get-togethers comes close to being a typical "dinner and a movie" date. In our opinion, a date is any occasion that lets you to get to know each other outside your usual environment. So free your mind of old-fashioned ideas, and take a cue from the suggestions below. Feel free to tweak the dialogue to make it your own. (We don't need to take credit for your suave sophistication. Your happiness is gratitude enough.)

Ask him to study. This is the most simple and innocent date. Figure out what he's good at—or figure out a subject that you might be able to help him with. Then snag him after class one day and pop the question. Example: "You really seem to get this sentence diagramming stuff. Do you have any time tonight to help me learn how to spot dangling participles?" This is also a risk-free date. If he meets you at the library and then spends the whole night talking about his ex-girlfriend, you can drop this guy from your crush files without losing face.

Ask him to be your project partner. One warning: Only attempt this date idea if your guy does well in the subject at hand. Don't risk a failing grade just to spend some Q.T. with a cutie. If your guy happens to excel at social studies (or whatever), then wait until the teacher suggests the class pairs off, and make your move. Example: "You have study hall eighth period, too, right? Why don't we be partners, and work on this project then?" With logic like that, he can't refuse. Library time leads to break time, break time leads to goofing around, and...well, the rest is up to you.

Ask him to dance. Your school is having its annual Winter Gala, and he's there and looking adorable. Use this casually festive setting to your advantage. Break free of your girlfriends and boogie over to your cutie. Then ask him to dance. Example: "Can you believe they're playing Madonna's 'Crazy for You'? I loved this song when I was like, seven. Want to dance?"

Ask him to meet you at a party. This is the closest you can get to asking him for a real date without actually doing so. As soon as you find out about the biggest party of the weekend, catch Loverboy in the lunch line and ask if he'll be there. Example:

"So, are you going to Jay's party Saturday night? Yeah, me, too. I'll be there around ten o'clock—look for me, okay?" You've smoothly turned a crowded bash into a private meeting, without once using the word "date."

(Ask him out alone.) This is about as traditional as you can get. And it'll be hard. Now, you might think it's easiest to ask him out in the comfort of your own bedroom, with you and a couple of your closest girlfriends on one end of your cordless phone and him on the other. Ditch that plan ASAP. Trust us when we tell you to go it alone. If he hears your pals whispering and giggling in the background, he's likely to think the whole thing is a big joke. Think about it. If the roles were reversed, you'd feel the same way.

If you can handle the face-to-face pressure, ask him in person. Telephone conversations, like e-mail, are less personal. So extend yourself, and your heart. Next time you and he are alone—say, washing the paint out of your brushes at the back of the art room—ask him out. Example: "If you aren't doing anything on Sunday, we should check out the town fair." The absolute worst thing he can say is "Sorry, can't. I've got plans already." And even then, he might suggest an alternate idea.

So, how do guys
really feel about
take-charge
girls?

*"It's always nice
for them to take
the first step, but
it doesn't stop me
if they don't."*
—Patrick

*"It's the best
thing in the world
when a girl makes
the first move.
We will almost
always say yes!"*
—Jeffrey

*"As long as we
like each other, it
doesn't matter
who does the ask-
ing."*
—Nicolas

*"I have to admit
I like aggressive
girls."*
—Antonio

THAT DIDN'T SOUND SO BAD, DID IT? When you take it apart, asking him out isn't all that intimidating.

We will admit, though, that being rejected is a possibility. Sometimes you may be head over heels for a guy who really does just want to be your friend.

So how will you feel when he turns you down? You can probably guess: dejected, sad, embarrassed.

But you know what? After you get over the shock of his negative answer, you may start to feel pretty proud of yourself. After all, you tried. That requires confidence. If you have the confidence to ask one guy out, you'll probably do it again. And the next guy you fall for might fall just as hard for you.

There may come a time when the wrong boy is interested in you. And though he may have spent weeks gathering his courage to ask you to the carnival, the sad fact is, you just don't feel as crazy about him as he does about you.

What's a girl to do? Let him down gracefully. Don't be mean by laughing in his face, or screaming "Eww, no!" Consider his feelings, and the courage it took to put his heart on the line. Tell him how it is: "Thanks, Jeff, but I can't. I think you're nice/smart/great, but I am interested in someone else right now." This way, his ego isn't shredded, and you won't feel evil when you flirt with his soccer buddy. You *did* tell him you liked someone else.

TWO'S COMPANY, AND SO IS A CROWD

Once you and he have agreed to go out on a date, the next logical step is deciding where and with whom. Often, it just seems more comfortable to get together in a multicouple group than to have a one-on-one. On the other hand, how annoying is it to watch him try to impress his guy friends by sticking a straw up his nose in the middle of a classy restaurant? And have you noticed how he rolls his eyes when you and your six best friends excuse yourselves to go to the ladies' room at the same time?

Each option has its own things going for it. The challenge is being able to predict which type of get-together suits you best.

GROUP ACTIVITIES

Skating at the ice rink, taking a day trip to the beach, getting together with the gang to see a blockbuster on opening night.

Pros:

a There's less pressure on the two of you to make conversation.

b Majority opinion rules the activities—you don't have to make all the decisions.

c You've got your friends with you in case of an emergency (you need gum, you realize you just got your period, you just decided you'll yak if he tries to kiss you, and so on).

43

Cons:

a When everyone else starts making out, there's more pressure on the two of you to do it, too.

b Every move either of you makes is being mentally recorded for later analysis by the more established couples in the gang.

c It's more difficult to have those refreshingly honest "all about me" conversations when his friends (or yours) are listening in.

SOLO VENTURES

Going out for dinner, playing miniature golf, seeing *Frankenstein* at the university (scary movies are great for holding hands!).

Pros:

a No one teases him when he puts his arm around you and gets his watch caught in your hair.

b You won't feel pressured to compete with more established couples in the make-out department.

c You can talk about Cocoa Puffs (or any other wacky thing you're both crazy about) for hours without anyone else yawning loudly.

Cons:

a Your friends aren't there to whisk you away and point out the green leaf that's been caught in your teeth since the salad course.

b When conversation dwindles to an awkward pause, you can't jump into another couple's conversation.

c There's more of an opportunity for unwanted sexual advances. (That last one shouldn't scare you, but it should remind you that a walk in the woods on a first date isn't the best idea.)

MONEY MATTERS

You should *never* be caught without enough cash to cover your half of the bill—with extra left over in case you need a taxi home. But once in a while you ought to pay for the whole date, too. The chart below will help you figure out who pays, and when.

YOU ask him out		
For a meal:	For a movie:	For an activity:
You pay. If he insists on paying, ask him to leave the tip. Or suggest he buy you ice cream at the shop up the block.	You both pay. He can buy the popcorn and snacks while you get the tickets.	You don't need to pay for his rental bowling shoes, but you should pay for the games.
HE asks you out		
He pays. But offer to leave the tip, or buy him a latte at the café down the street.	Let him buy the tickets, while you take over snack patrol.	Put him in charge of transportation and tickets. But while you're buying yourself a soda, get him one, too.
YOU meet with a group		
Splitting the bill fourteen ways will be a headache no matter what. Unless he shouts out, "How much for me and my date?" whip out your own wallet for this one.	Feel it out. If he suggests you get a seat with the other girls, leave the ticket-buying to him. If he holds your hand all the way to the window, ask him if he needs a ten.	You should each buy your own bunch of tickets at the amusement park. And if he buys the cotton candy at 2 P.M., you should pay for the ice cream at 4.

Chances are, if you've enjoyed a date with him, he's had a blast with you, too. And from there, phone and hallway encounters will certainly get easier. Pretty soon, you two will be taking it for granted that you've got plans every weekend, and your friends will tag your names together as if they are one (Kim-and-Ray). When your little sister starts challenging him to games of computer Candy Land, you'll know for sure that your relationship has really grown.

In fact, at right about that point you'll probably start asking yourself, "**SO, ARE WE BOYFRIEND AND GIRLFRIEND?**" If you need a little advice about **GETTING SERIOUS**, read on.

chapter 5

Getting Serious

I am sixteen years old. I have a relationship with this guy John. We've been together for about seven weeks, but we are not officially "boyfriend-girlfriend." When we got together we agreed to see other people, but now I think it's time for us to be boyfriend and girlfriend. What do I do?

If you stick with one boy long enough, you may be daydreaming in class one day and realize that you're aching to call him your boyfriend, and that you feel more than ready to **TAKE THE RELATIONSHIP TO A NEW LEVEL.**

Serious relationships are amazing. But in a way, they're like a really tough class: If you just show up, do your thing, and leave, it's unlikely you'll get ahead. You need to invest time, commitment, and emotion to be truly successful.

So how can you tell if you are ready? Let us help you figure it out. We'll show you how to find your way around certain love detours, and talk about exactly what makes a perfect couple.

RELATIONSHIP GLOSSARY

To avoid a misunderstanding between you and your babe, it makes sense to be on the same page as far as guy-girl terminology goes. So here's a rundown of some common phrases, in order of seriousness.

Went with: As in, "I went with him at the party last weekend." It means you two kissed, but didn't have an actual date. Other ways to say it: made out with, hooked up.

Together: As in, "He's not my boyfriend, we are just together right now." You've kissed and hung out, but if you meet a guy on spring break next week, you'll be free to kiss him, too.

Seeing each other: Slightly more serious than being together. In theory you can date other people, but there's usually a silent understanding that you won't.

Going out: The stage at which you can safely refer to him as your boyfriend. In general, kissing another person while you're going out with someone is cheating.

Dating: Chances are, you'll hear this classic phrase most from your parents and grandparents. (And from us, but that's just so we don't have to keep using the phrase "going out.") Other adorable old-fashioned phrases include: "Do you have a beau?" "Are you going with anyone these days?"

LOVE TIMELINE

Pacing a relationship is very personal. You probably know couples that met on a Friday night and said "I love you" by Monday. And you might know another couple that has been "seeing each other" and other people since you were in sixth grade. But no matter how long it takes you to go from a quick peck on the lips at a party to regular Saturday night dates, certain feelings can clue you in to the intensity of the relationship.

PHASE ONE: NERVOUSNESS

As things first start to heat up with you and your not-yet boyfriend, every single event or thought that has to do with him gives you major stomach butterflies. He touches you on the back as you walk up the staircase: butterflies. Your friends report that he was talking about you in class yesterday: butterflies. Your mom asks you how things are going with what's-his-name: butterflies. Being with this boy is thrilling, wonderful, and brand-new.

PHASE TWO: SEXINESS

Soon, however, those butterflies give way to an urge to kiss him and hug him every minute of every day. You want to sit as close to him as possible in assembly, wrap your arms around him as you walk home after school, and spend hours just kissing him and running your hands through his hair. Now you aren't so much nervous as you are anxious to be near him. You know him, you trust him, and you want to spend every minute of every day in his arms.

PHASE THREE: COZINESS

Once you two get comfortable around each other, and are more secure in the knowledge that each is gaga over the other, a certain mushy coziness sets in. It is at this stage of the relationship that friends might become a wee bit jealous. You and your guy have established a natural flow to your relationship: you hold hands on the way to class, kiss hello and good-bye, smile knowingly when people tell you how lucky you are to have each other, and generally seem like the perfect couple.

PHASE FOUR: COMPANIONSHIP

When you hit the companionship phase of a relationship, friends might accuse you of acting like an old married couple. The fact is, you have been together so long and care so deeply about each other that you don't need to kiss hello every time you see each other in the hallways. You aren't really acting like an old married couple—you're acting like best friends. Well, best friends who kiss. What could be better?

There's no rule that says a relationship has to progress beyond hanging out and kissing on Saturday nights and then talking once or twice during the week. You and your honey may have already decided you don't want things to get too serious. Or maybe you're dating him for fun, while waiting for your lifelong crush (whom you only see during summers at the shore) to fall in love with you.

Again, there is no rule. If you and your guy hit it off immediately, and spend two hours on the phone every night getting to know every last detail of each other's lives, you might very well consider him your best friend (and kissing partner) within a week's time. Or you might not.

So, how can you tell when it's time to get serious with your sweetie? Take this quiz to find out.

REALITY CHECK

ARE YOU READY FOR A SERIOUS RELATIONSHIP?

1 Your parents are hosting this year's family reunion. The guest list is limited to relatives and their spouses (read: your boyfriend isn't invited). You think

a This is a great excuse to avoid having him meet your parents.

b The restriction is bogus. You and he are dating, and you're definitely much more in love than your cousin Selma and her third husband.

c You'll have to arrange to sneak out of the reunion and meet him at the café for a late-night latte.

2 It's been exactly a month since you two first hooked up, and you'd like to celebrate by

a Heading over to Baskin Robbins with your friends to meet him and his pals, the way you do every Friday night.

b Treating him to a meal at Antonio's Trattoria. He's been picking up the tab for four weekends straight.

c Receiving his treasured basketball jersey, along with a sterling silver bracelet engraved with both of your initials.

3 Your guy asks you to watch his big game after school, but you already promised your friends you'd join them in a caramel sundae run to Friendly's. You tell him

a "Sure, but I'm leaving at half-time to get ice cream with Maria, Katie, and Lisa."

b "The girls and I are jonesing for sundaes. Sorry, babe."

c "Okay. Let me tell the girls that they'll have to go to Friendly's without me."

4 You and your best friend tag along with her older cousins to a night club. The four of you are busting a move on the dance floor when the cutest guy in the place starts grinding behind you. You react by

a Boogying away from him to the other side of your dancing circle. You're taken, thanks.

b Turning around and dancing with him for this song. Next song you'll introduce him to your single friend.

c Getting down with this hottie, and passing him your e-mail address at the end of the night. Well, it's not like you *kissed* him or anything.

5 It's Friday, and you and he haven't discussed weekend plans. When he stops by your locker after school to ask you what movie you want to see tonight, you reply

a "Sorry, I'm busy."

b "You want to rent some classics tonight? Let's watch the whole *Star Wars* trilogy."

c "Actually, I already told Michele and Phil we'd go mini-golfing with them. You don't mind, right?"

SCORING

1. a) 1   b) 3   c) 2
2. a) 1   b) 2   c) 3
3. a) 2   b) 1   c) 3
4. a) 3   b) 2   c) 1
5. a) 1   b) 2   c) 3

(13-15) Hopelessly Devoted

You really like this guy, that much is clear. And you may well be aching to declare your seriousness. But step back for one minute and think about this: Devotion is cool, but part of the responsibility of being in a relationship is making sure that it doesn't consume either one of you. You need to make time for yourself and your friends as well as being there for him. So chill a little: dance with whomever you please, let your guy suggest weekend plans every so often, and don't freak if your family doesn't treat him like an in-law. Oh—and the next time you're choosing between the girls or your guy, offer your sweetie your lucky troll doll for good luck at the game—you've got some ice cream to eat.

(9-12) Solidly Grounded

You feel pretty secure about his feelings and your own. And while you know his presence would make your family reunion a zillion times more tolerable, you also know that it won't kill you to be apart—it might even make your late-night rendezvous that much more thrilling. You've got your priorities in order, and have no intention of cutting off your friends, family, or even your precious alone time just because there's a boy in your life. And that's a sure sign that you are ready, willing, and able to get serious with him. So initiate the boyfriend-girlfriend conversation. He's probably been wondering when you'd mention it.

(5-8) Sketchily Undecided

You enjoy his company—on your terms. If it works out that the two of you get together over the weekend, you can dig it. But if something else comes up, you'll catch him next time. You're young, you know how many interesting people there are to meet, and you're in no rush to limit yourself. There's nothing wrong with this carefree philosophy, but for now, it doesn't make sense to get all caught up in heavy commitment chats with your guy. Serious relationships only work when you want them to. For you, right now, with him, a serious relationship isn't going to fly. Keep it light, until you decide you want to get serious.

LOVE DETOURS

You'd think that if you're sweating him and he's fallen for you, and you scored higher than a 9 on the quiz, then all systems would be go for a major thing between the two of you. But alas, Juliet, there might just be something or someone preventing you and Romeo from becoming the most envied couple in school. Luckily, if you encounter any of these obstacles, you'll know how to overcome them. Check it out:

LOVE DETOUR №1:

Another girl wants your guy.

Q *My boyfriend's brother has a friend (a girl) who flirts with my boyfriend. She won't leave him alone, though I've asked her to lots of times. What should I do?*

A No girl is going to listen to the girlfriend of the boy she's after. Don't waste your time warning her away from your guy. Instead, first make sure that he isn't encouraging her behavior. Then let him know that her attention bothers you. Explain to him that, though he can be friends with whomever he chooses, it makes you feel pretty small when she worms her way in between the two of you—literally—and engages him in an AB conversation (as in, C you later).

(LOVE DETOUR №2:)

Your friends hate him, or vice versa.

Q *My boyfriend is great with me, but he just can't seem to get along with my friends. My friends are asking me to choose, and I don't know what to do.*

A If he's butting heads with your pals, he needs to decide which is more important: his feelings for your friends, or his feelings for you. Ask him to make an effort to like your buds. And ask them to either come up with a good reason for giving him such a hard time, or declare a truce, for your sake.

(LOVE DETOUR №3:)

He lives far away.

Q *My boyfriend just found out his dad got a new job, and his family is moving to another state. He said we can make a long-distance relationship work, but I am not sure.*

A Long-distance relationships are very hard to sustain. But you can keep it fresh by maintaining a steady communication. Write him letters and e-mails and talk on the phone as often as your budget and time allow. Fill each other in on important and trivial stuff: the hangnail you got while rescuing a baby bird from a fallen nest, his record time running the 100-yard dash, the oral report you aced in public-speaking class. If you make an effort to keep each other updated on your lives, it'll be easier to reconnect when you finally get together.

LOVE DETOUR №4:

You have major differences.

Q *I met this incredible guy. We have so much in common; the only problem is that he's black and I'm white. My parents don't approve, but I know they'd love him if they took time to get to know him. How can I make them see past his color?*

A If you two are willing to look past certain differences (such as race or religion) and see each other as complete people, then the relationship has a strong chance of survival. If outside influences—like your parents—are ruining your love groove, you need to address that. Sit down with them for a heart-to-heart. Tell them what makes your guy so special and wonderful. With a little help from you, chances are they'll come around.

LOVE DETOUR №5:

One of you isn't allowed to date.

Q *Help! My boyfriend can't see me anymore because his parents think he's too young to have a relationship. How can he make them understand how we feel?*

A We aren't going to tell you to sneak around this rule by getting together in large groups and then pairing off with your sweetie. No way. Instead, we suggest you try compromising with the overprotective parents: Agree to go on double dates, and only after his parents have spent time—on their own turf—with you and your guy. Surely they'll be flexible when they see how you've confronted their concerns in a mature manner.

KEEPING IT REAL

Have you agreed on dating definitions? Taken the quiz and realized you are determined to be one half of the perfect couple? Gone around every love detour standing in your way? If so, then you and your sweetie are officially boyfriend and girlfriend. (Of course, you've already discussed it with him, right?) But being a girlfriend means living up to certain expectations. And it means expecting certain things from your guy, too. Here are a few key elements you'll both need to work on continually:

Communication: The best way to keep up a healthy relationship is by communicating. And we don't just mean calling each other promptly at 8:15 every night to whisper sweet nothings over the fiber-optic phone lines. As we've already mentioned, relationships take work. For instance, say your boyfriend and you get in a big fight over how you like your bagel toasted. (Hey, it happens.) And within minutes you've gone from screaming about burned bagels to blaming him for your D in algebra. And then, after he gets through listing your annoying quirks, like how you pick through the bag of chips to find the cheesiest Doritos, he storms away. What should you do?

a Cry a little and wait for him to call you.
b Cry a little and think about his side of things, then call to discuss your new thoughts.

c Cry a little and decide it's time to break up.

Choice b) reflects the actions of a girl who wants to make a relationship work. Communication means talking through arguments, it means letting him know when you're feeling jealous or insecure (*without* blaming him—unless it really is his fault), and it means telling him how much you care about him. And it means that you should be hearing the same things from him.

Free will: No, you don't have to bake him chocolate chip cookies before every big game. And he doesn't have to spend his gas station earnings buying you the Led Zeppelin BBC disc set you've been dying for. Neither of you has to do *anything* for the other person—unless you want to.

Devotion is lovely, if you have a dog or a cat. But with people, free will is essential. Never do anything for your guy because you think he "expects" you to. Isn't it nicer to get flowers on any old day rather than on Valentine's Day or your birthday? That's because there was no prompting, hint-dropping or "I have to" involved—just a spontaneous act of love.

Sense of self: He likes you because you are you, and you like him for the very same reason. And since you followed our advice and used your natural charisma to catch his eye, why would you change now? Don't suffer through hours of football every Sunday for seventeen weekends straight if you'd rather be perfecting your tennis backhand.

And just as you wouldn't want to make yourself over for his sake, you shouldn't try to change him. He may never feel the eerie chill that you do while watching a particularly good *X-Files* episode, but that's just fine. Because when you call him after the show's over, he can entertain you with stories of what he did all night.

(Independence:) It's easy to get caught up in the roller-coaster emotions of a serious relationship. And it's natural to want to spend as much time as possible talking with, cuddling with, and making out with your boyfriend. You've waited for moments like these! But you can't neglect the rest of your life to do so.

If you moon over him instead of studying the night before a big exam, you're going to fail. And if you blow off your girlfriends every weekend to spend more quality time with your guy, you're going to lose your friends. Furthermore, there are probably just so many times your mom will forgive you for not picking up your little brother from nursery school before she grounds you. The best way to make a good relationship even stronger is for both of you to keep up with the other people and activities in your lives, while also making time for each other.

SEVEN SIGNS YOU'RE BOTH TOO CLINGY

1 The two of you get detention for committing a dozen PDA (public-display-of-affection) offenses in one week.

2 You just found out from your math teacher that your best friend sprained her ankle in gym class—*last week.*

3 His mother is caught off guard on the one night you *don't* come over for dinner.

4 His coach checks with *you* to find out if your honey will be at baseball practice today.

5 He decides to forgo the soccer team's spring-break trip to sunny Miami Beach, Florida, because he can't stand to be without you for three whole days.

6 His friends have started calling him "Bubba bear"—your pet name for him.

7 Your friends have gone from calling you the Dynamic Duo to the Gruesome Twosome.

CHECKLIST OF GIRLFRIEND RIGHTS

With the title "girlfriend" come certain responsibilities and privileges (gee, don't you feel like Miss Teen USA?). Scope out these situations, and ✓ **CHECK OFF** the reaction you'd most likely have. **BE HONEST, NOW!**

Here's the deal	It's cool if you	But come on,
While on the phone with you, he gets a beep, answers it, and comes back to you minutes later.	✓ Ask him who called, if you are curious. Just bear in mind that he might be just as inquisitive when you get call waiting.	○ Don't tell him he can't get calls from his female lab partner. You are both free to have friends of the opposite sex.
He and the guys are trying to get into an over-twenty-one nightclub.	○ Tell him you're worried that he'll get arrested for using fake identification.	✓ You can't forbid him to go. But you can let him know you think it's a dumb idea.
His dad gave him two tickets to the hottest concert of the year, and both you and his best friend are major fans.	○ Express how much you'd love to go to the concert. And remind him that the band does play "your" song.	✓ Don't threaten drastic consequences if he takes his best friend. He made his choice. But suggest that next time, you get preference.
He's visiting an out-of-state college on your six-month anniversary weekend.	✓ Mention that you are upset he'll be missing the big day. Then suggest you celebrate the weekend before or after.	○ Chill. He's prioritizing properly. College is a life-changing decision, whereas an anniversary is not a life-changing event.
Your best friend saw your boyfriend at a party in the next town, getting cozy with another girl.	✓ Run this story past him. She may have misunderstood what she saw, but he still needs to explain.	○ Don't freak out on him before listening to his side—it's unfair and shows that you have little trust in a guy you care about.

CHECKLIST OF BOYFRIEND RIGHTS

Now ✓ **CHECK OFF** the reactions you think he'd have. And feel free to read aloud from this chart whenever you feel he's crossing the line.

Here's the deal	It's cool if he	But come on,
Some freshman guy booed your violin solo, and your boyfriend wants to defend your honor.	⊘ Tells you how much he wants to shut that pip-squeak up.	◯ There's no reason to get physical when putting a lid on the wiseguy. Nobody deserves a busted nose.
Your single girl friends want you to come out dancing Friday night.	◯ Reminds you that he's your one and only before you go.	⊘ He should *not* have veto power over your tight/short/sexy outfit.
You twist your ankle in gym class, and a cute senior gives you a piggyback ride off the field. Your honey hears about this chivalrous act secondhand.	◯ Asks you what you were doing on the shoulders of the class president.	⊘ Once he hears your explanation, he should be all about getting ice for your ankle, and *not* about being jealous.
You call him to cancel a date after your best friend calls. Her guy broke up with her and she's devastated.	◯ Lets his disappointment show. He's been planning this lakeside picnic all week.	⊘ He shouldn't throw a fit. After all, he'd want you to understand if he needed to be there for his friend, right?
Between soccer, kickboxing, and your reading group, you haven't been able to fit him in all week.	◯ Asks you what's up. If you can make time for *I Love Lucy* reruns, surely you can make time for him.	◯ He can't ask you to quit an activity. And he'd better not tell you to. (But you *could* try prioritizing a bit better.)

MYSTERIES OF THE DATING WORLD

Once you get a boyfriend, odd changes occur in your social life, your ability to attract other guys, and your relationship with your friends. Is there a logical explanation for these dating phenomena? Why yes, there is.

STRANGE BUT TRUE: As soon as you have a boyfriend, every male you come in contact with suddenly wants your phone number.

While you might wonder if you're emitting some sort of radar signal that draws all boys straight to you, this is really another case of the power of self-confidence. Now, we're not saying you need a boyfriend to make you a confident, happy person. But it does make sense that if you are able to communicate and get along with your boyfriend, then you will be comfortable talking to any guy. And when you're comfortable, you are at your most appealing.

The moral of this story, of course, is that if you can feel comfortable with guys all the time—and not just when you're in a committed relationship—you'll be a year-round guy magnet.

STRANGE BUT TRUE: When you have a boyfriend, your single friends look to you as their relationship guru.

It doesn't matter that you and your sweetie have only been going out for fifteen days. Now your friends come to you for advice on whether to return their crush's e-mail as soon as they read it or wait until the weekend's over. They consider you the expert on what to do with your tongue while his is busy poking around in your mouth. And they want you to share every detail of your romantic life, so that they can learn.

Flattering? Sure. It's nice to be thought of as an authority on a subject. So share your wisdom (skipping the most personal details), but remind your friends that everyone does things a bit differently, and while being coy or keeping your tongue in your own mouth may work for you, they might choose a different approach.

STRANGE BUT TRUE: You're invited places you've never been before.

Your friendship base has doubled to include his friends as well as your own. And now you're swapping lipstick with the eleventh-grade girls who never even blessed your sneezes before you started dating him, and you're going to Honor Society socials even though your GPA is, well, not quite worthy of membership.

It's awesome to be able to choose between parties on the weekends, and to chat it up with new people. Yet every so often— like when you sneeze—you remember that the only reason they're saying "Bless you" is because you're dating a guy in their crowd. This might make you a little cranky. But don't give in to the funk. Remember, they *had* to get to know you because you're dating their friend, but they don't *have* to like you. And they *do* like you.

"I stopped checking out other guys."
—Amber

"I wasn't as outgoing. I spent too much time around my house waiting for him to call, which wasn't a good thing."
—Beth

"I cared less what other people thought of me."
—Karissa

"I became more popular, and got out of the house more."
—Kristina

"My social life improved, and I made new friends—his friends."
—Brooke

SWEET TEMPTATIONS

Just when you're feeling completely secure in your relationship, temptation rears its ugly little head in the form of gossip, jealousy, or another cutie. If you know what to look out for, however, you can squash temptation like the nasty little gnat it is, and get on with your love life.

TEMPTATION №1: KISS AND TELL

It's so hard to resist giving your pals a detailed play-by-play of your twenty-minute make-out session, or the exact spot in the movie where he cried. But resist you must. It's cool to let your friends know that he tried to go to second base and you turned him down—if you feel like sharing that information. But it's not cool to analyze every single sweet nothing that led up to that moment. Keep some things private, and they'll remain special between you and your honey.

TEMPTATION №2: JUMPING TO CONCLUSIONS

He doesn't call you after being out with his friends all day. It can only mean that he met another girl and is spending the evening scamming on you, right? No, silly. But it's not unusual for your insecurities to make you imagine things like this. Everybody—boys included—has these thoughts.

Sometimes it's easier to picture the worst-case scenario than it is to imagine a realistic situation. (Like when you're a half hour past curfew and your mom imagines you've been in a fatal car accident, when really you just couldn't find anyone to drive you home.) But after your mind plays this horror movie through, your common sense should take over and remind you that your boyfriend cares about you enough to respect your feelings. And later, he'll probably explain that the only pay phone was covered in gum. Ick.

TEMPTATION №3: SHOPPING AROUND

Going out with a guy isn't the same as being married to him. But it is still a commitment. You've told him you won't see anyone else, and it's important that you stay true to your word. For instance, if you're visiting your sister at college and meet a good-looking university boy at the campus bookstore, it really isn't fair to your boyfriend to have coffee with College Boy without mentioning up front that you're in a relationship. If you find yourself checking out other boys more often than you daydream about your own, it might be time to split up. But if you still consider your guy to be quite a catch, relax. It's healthy to notice other guys. Just don't give them your phone number.

There's just one more thing before we close this chapter. At some point in a relationship, whether you've been dating him for a month or a year, you'll encounter a gift-giving holiday. Whether it's a birthday, an anniversary, Valentine's Day or Hanukkah, you need to be prepared. The chart on the next page can help.

	Birthday	Anniversary	Christmas/ Hanukkah/ Kwanzaa	Valentine's Day
1 month in; phone calls three times a week	His very own copy of *South Park, the movie*.	A goody bag filled with his favorite candy and junk food.	A milk crate filled with home-made goodies and knickknacks.	A funny card and a tray of his favorite blond brownies.
1 month in; phone calls daily	A tub of surf-board wax and a new board leash (or some other sporty accessory).	Your treat at the new sushi joint in town.	A biography of his hero, Michael Jordan.	A sappy card, his favorite brownies, and a single rose.
3 months in; never met his parents	A baseball cap and T-shirt of his favorite sports team.	A full day of fun for two at the nearest amuse-ment park.	A video game cartridge.	A pair of cheesy "xoxo" boxer shorts and a box of chocolates.
3 months in; his little sister worships you	Tickets to the concert he's been dying to go to.	A framed photo/ticket stub/greeting card collage.	A long-sleeved knit shirt to bring out the color of his eyes.	Six red roses and a gift certificate to the sporting goods store.
6 months in; you still get stomach butterflies	An autographed Pittsburgh Steelers' jersey.	A homemade coupon booklet, good for things like backrubs.	A vintage Swiss Army watch that you found at a junk shop.	Silk boxers (even if you've never seen him in a bathing suit).
6 months in; you're like best friends	Subscriptions to *ESPN The Magazine*, *SPIN*, and *Details*.	Dinner at a très chic French bistro, your treat.	A holiday memento (like a tree ornament) and a sweater.	Ski gear for the upcoming class ski weekend.

ROMANTIC RELATIONSHIPS ROCK. He's a boy, he's your friend, and you can kiss him anytime you want. How great is that? And if you can survive some of the relationship hurdles described in this chapter, you're probably meant to be together.

chapter 6

The Real Deal

I have a question. How can I know, when my boyfriend and I say "I love you" to each other, that we really mean it?

LOVE IS MAJOR. You love your mom, you love your dog, you love your best friend. But *falling in love* feels so far removed from those kinds of love. Your feelings for him are so intense, it's often overwhelming.

It can be hard to tell the difference between being in love, being in like, and being in lust. All of those dizzy states make you feel happy, crazy, and exhausted at the same time. So how can you know when you're *really* in love?

For starters, love usually works both ways. Having an intense, all-consuming crush on a boy may feel powerful enough to be love, but if you don't really know him at all, you probably aren't in love with him—you're infatuated. To love someone, you need to really know him. And there is a big difference between knowing all about someone and actually *knowing* someone. For instance, you may have memorized everything about Leonardo DiCaprio after *Titanic* came out, but you don't really *know* him, do you? (And if you do, could you introduce us?)

It's also easy to get confused between being in love with a person and loving being in a relationship. Of course you love having a boyfriend—if you don't, you're with the wrong guy. Relationships add another dimension to your already full life. And having a boyfriend can make you feel very special. But if you can't tell whether you are in love with the circumstance or the actual person you are dating, wait a while before announcing your loving feelings.

Do you feel as if you might be in love with your boyfriend? Choose the best answer to these situations to gain deeper insight into your own heart.

REALITY CHECK

IS IT LOVE?

1 He walks into a room and you get
a Smiley.
b Horny.
c Queasy.

2 Your friends start talking about your guy at lunch and you gush

- **a** "Mmm, he is such a good kisser."
- **b** "He is so fine. Don't you think he's the cutest guy in our grade?"
- **c** "Last night we were on the phone for hours. I don't even know what we talked about."

3 You're going away for a week. To remind yourself of him you bring

- **a** Your favorite picture of him—sometimes you forget exactly what he looks like.
- **b** His sweater, which you will wear as a reminder that you've got someone waiting at home.
- **c** A love letter he wrote you, so it's like you're hearing him speak to you every time you read it.

4 When you daydream about him, your visions are filled with

- **a** Images of the two of you at the senior prom.
- **b** Passionate kisses and sexy hugs.
- **c** Scenes of the two of you in a cozy garden apartment.

5 He's late meeting you at a house party. You jump to conclusions by thinking

- **a** He's ditched you.
- **b** He's hooking up en route with his best girl friend.
- **c** He's been in a terrible accident.

SCORING

1. a) 3 b) 2 c) 1
2. a) 2 b) 1 c) 3
3. a) 2 b) 1 c) 3
4. a) 2 b) 1 c) 3
5. a) 2 b) 1 c) 3

(13-15) In love

Thinking of him makes you grin. You'd rather not carry pictures of him around because they're no substitute for the real thing. You could kiss him for hours, but you'd be just as happy snuggling, chatting, or giggling with him. You are in love, sister, and your first concern when he's late is for his well-being. You've gone through infatuation, you've been in like, and you know that your feelings for your guy are deeper than the wishing well at the park.

(9-12) In like

You are hot for your boy, and you don't care who knows it. When he touches your arm, you get shivers up your spine. You daydream about his kisses, and imagine what it would be like to just hug all day. You are in serious like, and that's only a step away from love. The difference? You still don't know all there is to know about your honey, and you'd like him to learn more about you. Take your time getting to know each other, and learn to believe him when he tells you he'd rather be with you than with any of the *Baywatch* babes. True love comes out of many things—physical attraction included—but one of the most important is trust. And that comes with time.

(5-8) In lust

You get nauseated (in a good way!) just thinking about him. You feel a crazy thrill when you pick up a warm pen he's been writing with, and you get all tingly when you pass a boy in the hall who wears the same cologne as your guy. You are hooked.

HERE'S THE DEAL: Lust is like the feeling you get during the first major loop on a roller coaster. It's exhilarating and fantastic, but after the third loop, the anticipation and thrill subsides, making way for sheer enjoyment. That's the "in like" phase—are you following? And if you're still digging the ride after you know its twists and turns by heart, then you're in it for the long haul. That, friends, is love.

TALKING THE TALK

I am sixteen years old and have been in a relationship for seven months. I am afraid what he would think if I told him I love him. I don't want him to totally freak out, but I want him to know.

So you think you love him. And you hope he loves you. But even if he doesn't, you'll burst if you don't tell him how you feel. Maybe it will inspire him to reveal his true feelings as well.

No matter which one of you takes that leap of faith and reveals their loving feelings first, it's scary. And it's often hard to formulate a complete sentence when you are a) about to lay your heart in his hands or b) stricken with the thought that though you're flattered that he loves you, you just don't feel the same way.

There are a few different ways the "I love you" talk can start. Imagine yourself in the following situations, and you'll be prepared for whatever happens.

You say it first, by mistake: He's meeting you at the mall, and as he walks towards you he waves, bumping into a woman with a stroller in the process. As he fumbles to help her gather her shopping bags, he apologizes profusely. When he finally catches up to you, you stop laughing long enough to giggle "I love you."

Say that again? Hey, it just slipped out. You didn't mean it *that* way, right? He probably realizes that. So unless he gives you a great big bear hug and says "I love you, too," buy yourself a Slurpee to help you cool off and then carry on with your shopping excursion.

You say it first, for real: You can't bring yourself to tell him to his face, so you do it over the phone. As he's getting ready to say good-bye, you suck in your breath and rush "I love you, bye."

Say that again? Okay, that was kind of a chicken move. Because you know he's going to be like "What'd you say?" After that, he may say "I love you, too" (and then you can breathe again) or he may be like "Okay, me too." The "Me too" phrase usually means the person has to give this matter some thought before repeating the L word back to you. Give it time. Before you know it, he'll bring it up again, and this time he'll be sure.

He says it first, by mistake: Who could blame him? You are pretty irresistible, especially when you're telling a story and you get so excited about it that your story takes off in a million different directions. After staring at you with a glazed expression for twenty minutes, it's no wonder he blurted out, "I love you."

Say that again? Don't wig out. Take it as a supreme compliment, smile, and continue your train of thought. If you've been waiting for him to say it, don't roll your eyes and say "Yeah, right!" or do anything else that might lead him to mistakenly believe that you don't feel the same.

He says it first, for real: He walks you home after you've spent eight hours at his house, watching a *Real World* marathon on MTV. When you reach for your house keys, he reaches for your arm and says, "I love you."

Say that again? Obviously, if you feel the same way, you should stop your key search and return the sentiment. Then you'll probably share a mushy moment and a kiss. If, however, you don't feel the same, you can pull the old "Me too" or personalize it by saying "Oh, babe, I care so much for you, too."

No matter who says it first, or why, there is one nonnegotiable rule in the game of love: You should NEVER say "I love you" if you don't mean it. It's not nice to lie about something so significant. You may convince yourself that you are sparing his feelings, but leading him on is just plain cruel. And telling a boy you love him so

"When you can overlook the stupid things he does and just smile."
—Veronica

"If you can't picture yourself without that person."
—Liz

"When you are together and you have so much fun, and you can see a future with this person."
—Katie

"When the kiss sets off fireworks inside you, and you can't stop thinking about him, even after a couple of months."
—Becky

you can get your own way (like you want him to give you his football jacket, or you're hoping he'll take you to the prom) is manipulative. Saying "I love you" is a *big deal*. Save it for when you really mean it, from the bottom of your heart.

DANGEROUS OBSESSIONS

It sounds like a movie of the week, doesn't it? The fact is, though, it could become the story of your life, if you get love confused with obsession. Some girls get so wrapped up in the lives of their boyfriends that they lose themselves completely. Perhaps you know a girl like this. Here are some warning signs:

1 She drops all of her other friends.

2 She changes her class schedule to more closely match her boyfriend's. Maybe she even took up metalworking class and dropped her favorite ceramics class.

3 She got a job at the same place her boyfriend works, or simply quit her own part-time job so she could spend more time with him.

4 She eats burgers with him at lunch every day—even though she used to be a vegetarian.

5 When you ask her to get together on a weekend afternoon, she tells you she doesn't want to leave her house because her guy's out of town, and he promised he'd call sometime today.

Why does this happen to some girls and not all? Tough question, and one that we can't fully answer without a degree in psychology. But we can tell you this: The very worst thing you can do to yourself and your relationship is to become obsessed with it. It is serious stuff. You should never make any one person or thing the focus of your existence. In fact, when it comes right down to it, you should always be the most important thing in your life. Your likes, dislikes, and schedule count just as much as—if not more than—your boyfriend's.

In order to avoid the obsession trap, make an effort to spend time doing your favorite activities and seeing your favorite people—other than him. And if you feel yourself becoming overwhelmed by your feelings for a boy, talk to someone—like a good friend—about it before you get in too deep. Because obsession and love are NOT the same thing.

(Here's the real thing to remember:) Love is a splendid thing, but it doesn't have to be the ultimate goal of every relationship you begin. Even if your boyfriend doesn't turn out to be the love of your life, you should enjoy your time together and have a blast. If you spend too much time analyzing the relationship and figuring out whether you care for him in the exact same way that he cares about you, the whole romance will lose steam and spontaneity. So go with the flow, and TRUST YOUR INSTINCTS.

Emotional closeness isn't the only tricky part of relationships. Another huge part of being in a romantic relationship is getting physical. In fact, some people go straight to the physical stuff before even deciding if they have anything in common besides instant attraction.

Though there may be times when you make out with a boy first and ask questions later, it really isn't a mature way to start a relationship. So now that we've talked about serious relationships and the possibility of love, we're ready to discuss KISSES AND ALL THE REST OF THAT STUFF. Are you?

chapter 7

Covering All Bases

I am sixteen and have never messed around with a guy before. I haven't met anyone I want to kiss—until now! He is so cool, and I want to kiss him so bad, but I am nervous.

You're probably wondering why we waited six whole chapters to talk about fooling around, when most of your classmates start kissing way before they become boyfriend-girlfriend. Good point. But there's a reason we gave you the tools for cementing a solid relationship with a guy first.

We'd like to think that you are not just a kissing bandit, and that you'd like to know how to flirt with him, ask him out, and express your feelings clearly before you learn how to play tonsil hockey.

Kissing is a lot of fun, and it's a nice way to feel close to someone. And we get so many letters from readers who aren't quite sure how to get started smooching, we figure a little guidance couldn't hurt.

But even though we have some kissing tips, this really isn't a how-to book. Fooling around is a natural part of being in a relationship, but where your idea of fooling around might be a little kissing, someone else may feel more comfortable going further. That's where this book comes in. Getting intimate with a boy is serious business, and it requires some serious thought. Every action has consequences, and part of being in a mature relationship is taking responsibility for your actions. We're here to help you decide whether you're ready to handle that kind of responsibility.

SCORING AT FIRST BASE

I'm fifteen, and I've never French-kissed anyone. I am so afraid that I will do it wrong. Please save me the embarrassment by telling me what to do, exactly.

It's completely normal to be nervous the first time you kiss a boy—whether he's the first guy you've ever kissed or just the latest in a string of boys. There are certain combinations that guarantee success, and others that scream failure. If you learn how to tell the difference, at least one of you will be prepared.

THE GOOD

Your slightly parted lips + his softly tilted head = a gentle, satisfying smooch without squished noses.

A prekiss sip of Sprite + a garlic-free meal = a fresh connection.

A few moments alone + a mutual attraction = a sweet encounter.

THE BAD

His open mouth + your closed smacker = a painful collision between his teeth and your lips.

Doritos + iced coffee = breath not even your dog would sniff.

Your gang of friends + a crowded school hallway = a high-pressure, low-pleasure smack.

THE UGLY

Your hands pushing against his chest + his hand forcing your head toward his = a forceful situation you need to get out of.

Your gently opened mouth + his tongue darting back and forth like a rabid dog = your first and last kiss with this guy.

Both of your drool + his stubble = a chin rash that will make you wince.

ROOM FOR IMPROVEMENT

Just because one kiss was bad, it doesn't mean his technique can't be corrected. If you're intent on swapping spit with this boy again, you can guide him to plant one on you the right way. These kissing tips can help:

1 If he orders a meal with garlic, onions, or any other strong-smelling ingredient, have a bite. If you both eat it, you won't taste it on each other's breath.

2 Let him lean into the kiss first. You can assess which way he's tilting his head, and respond in kind, avoiding a head-on crash.

3 Breathe through your nose. It's scary to have to pull away gasping for air because you forgot to breathe altogether.

4 If drool collects on your face (and we won't say whose drool), just bring your hand to your mouth when you disengage, and wipe your chin swiftly and casually.

5 The whole joined-at-the mouth braces myth is just a myth. But avoid cutting your tongue on his metal apparatus by staying between his teeth.

A KISS
IS JUST A KISS

OR IS IT? Check out our kissing chart to pair the intensity and type of kiss with the situation.

Situation	Type of kiss	Respectable duration
He's walked you to class and the bell is about to ring.	A soft peck: lips slightly parted; no tongue.	Two to three seconds. A floor show won't score points with your teacher.
Your best friend gave him a lift home, and he's leaning over the front seat to say good-bye to you.	A chaste smack. Remember kissing Grandma when you were three? Yeah—like that.	Spend about as much time kissing him good-bye in these close quarters as you do blinking.
The two of you are alone in the hallway at a friend's no-parents party.	Feel free to French. You can even fall into a dramatic hand-on-back-of-neck embrace, if the mood strikes.	No longer than two minutes. Party-goers are sure to pass through on the way to the bathroom.
The movie theater is dark and you're sitting in the back row.	A cinematic smooch: all loose lips, no tongue swapping.	Don't drag this on past the opening credits. Enjoy a semiprivate kiss, then enjoy the action on the big screen.
Your parents are out to dinner, and the two of you are watching old movies at your house.	Indulge in a little nonstop make-out. But only go as far as you feel comfortable.	No time limits—just make sure you allow yourself time to reapply lip gloss before your parents walk in the door.

THE RUMOR MILL

Naturally, you want to fool around and kiss your sweetie all the time. You probably also want to talk about it with your friends. Which is fine, as long as you don't divulge every last detail at the lunch table.

Remember the telephone game, where you make up a story and whisper it in the ear of the person to your right? As it slowly makes its way around the room, whispered from ear to ear, it changes, and by the time it gets back to you it bears only the slightest resemblance to the story you originally made up. That's a rumor. And the more personal info you share—even if it's only with your closest friends—the more likely a rumor will circulate about you. Don't believe us? Read on:

While waiting to buy a turkey sub on the lunch line, you whisper to your best friend that your boyfriend tried—unsuccessfully—to unbutton your blouse last night.

Your arch rival from art class overhears, and runs back to her table to report that you let your boyfriend get to second base last night.

A girl at the table is dating a guy on your boyfriend's soccer team. She tells her guy that you took off your blouse for your boyfriend last night.

He tells a few of his teammates that you did a striptease for your boyfriend last night.

Your boyfriend shows up to the locker room for soccer practice after school and gets pats on the back for scoring with you last night. His buddies want to know what it was like to lose his virginity.

Your boyfriend calls you that night to find out exactly what you've been telling people, especially considering you didn't even let him near your shirt!

In a matter of hours, you've become a nonvirgin. And all you did was fill your best friend in on the specifics of your make-out session. The lesson: Discretion is a wonderful thing.

DOING IT RIGHT

I've been dating my boyfriend for about five months, and he's ready for sex. I am a virgin and so is he. I love him a lot and he says he loves me. He also says he wants me to be his first. Should I trust him and go along with it?

The decision to have sexual intercourse with someone is a huge deal, and one that is totally up to you. Not to get all preachy, but having sex with a person is about as intimate as you can get. Not only are you taking a giant emotional leap, you are risking pregnancy and a variety of unpleasant and damaging STDs (sexually transmitted diseases), including HIV. Because, as your parents and teachers have probably told you about a million times, the only way to completely prevent STDs and pregnancy is to not have sex *at all*.

Even if you take all the proper health precautions (using condoms plus another form of birth control is a good place to start), you need to be sure you're having sex for the right reasons. Doing it because your boyfriend thinks it's about time is a bad reason. When we said that this decision is yours alone to make, we meant it. Absolutely. You should never, ever have sex with a person if you have any doubts.

So why have sex at all? The human body is programmed to enjoy physical contact. That's why, when you hug your honey, you want to press so close you melt right into him. It just feels nice. People become sexually active for a variety of reasons, but the best one we can think of is because they feel they are in a loving, committed relationship with a person they trust fully. And they want to do it, rather than feeling they have to.

So why wait? Because it can take a long time to figure out whether you are in the kind of relationship that will grow and support the powerful feelings that come with being sexually intimate. You have your whole life to make this decision. And once you do have sex with someone, you can't pretend it didn't happen. If you know you aren't ready to deal with the complications that having sex can produce (like unwanted pregnancy or disease, or guilt or rejection), then it makes sense to wait until you are certain you can handle it.

REALITY CHECK

ARE YOU READY FOR SEX?

1 You have the best time with this guy, whether you're studying, partying, talking or kissing.   True/False

2 Your friends have suggested you have sex before the summer/prom/college so that you'll be able to enjoy it by then. After all, practice makes perfect.   True/False

3 You've memorized the whole "condom plus another form of birth control" rule, and plan to follow it.   True/False

4 You can't even imagine what you'd do if you ever got pregnant. True/False

5 Aside from your best friend since kindergarten, you consider your sweetheart to be your closest pal.   True/False

6 He doesn't know you're a virgin.   True/False

7 He's told you everything about his sexual past and STD screenings.   True/False

8 You probably won't go to the gynecologist unless you need birth control pills.   True/False

9 You've been thinking about having sex with him for weeks now. True/False

10 You'll probably have a drink to loosen up before your first time with him.   True/False

SCORING

You should have answered True for every odd-numbered statement and **False for every even number**. If you scored:

10 out of 10: Well, you've definitely done your homework, and you've clearly given sex a lot of thought. But you can never be too sure—so why not think about this a little more before taking action. Better safe than sorry, right?

8 out of 10: Brush up on your STD prevention knowledge and really think about what you'd do if you did get pregnant. Then take another pass at the quiz and reevaluate your feelings.

6 out of 10: You need to ponder this decision for a while longer. In the meantime, talk to your honey about his sexual past and his feelings for you. The world won't end if you make a decision you eventually regret, but wouldn't it be nicer if you never regret your first time?

5 or less out of 10: You are not ready. Get yourself on the Planned Parenthood Web site and research sexual health, then sit down for a long chat with your sweetie. Finally, examine the driving force behind your desire to have sex. Don't rush into it just because you think you're the only virgin left in school. Having sex is not a chore, or a hurdle to get past. It is a mature act requiring mature thought.

THE POWER OF PERSUASION

I passed a guy my number, and he called me. We got together at his place, and took a nap in his bed. When we woke up, he wanted to have sex, but I said no. I think he got mad, because afterward he wouldn't call me again. What is his problem?

You may already know that you aren't ready for sex. And while many boys will respect your decision, there are guys who, for one reason or another, will try to convince you to see things their way. Rather than get upset or, worse yet, give in to persuasion, use some of the solid ways we've come up with to let him know that no means no.

He says: "You would if you loved me."
You say: "No. You wouldn't ask if you loved me. I've already told you how much I care for you, but I've also told you that I don't want to have sex with you yet."

He says: "But if you don't, I'll be in so much pain."
You say: "Didn't we cover this in health class? You may feel a little frustrated for a few minutes, but my saying 'no' isn't going to cause permanent damage down there."

He says: "Rob and Jenna have done it, and so have Lisa and Todd."

You say: "Okay, but I'm not Jenna or Lisa, and I think that's why you went out with me in the first place, right? I'm not ready yet."

He says: "You are a total tease."

You say: "If you get cranky every time we fool around without having sex, then maybe we just shouldn't fool around."

And that concludes our lecture for today. Honestly, we won't judge you—whatever you decide. But we do encourage you to know your own limits and refuse to let yourself be pressured into going farther than you want. It's a personal decision, and what's right for your older sister or your best friend is not necessarily what's right for you. So think about it, and discuss it with people you trust, like your boyfriend, your best friend—even your parents or a close relative, if you feel comfortable doing that.

After reading this chapter, you'll probably become not only the best kisser in your grade (unless your classmates have also been reading this book), but also an expert at refusing a pushy boy. What we most want you to remember, however, is the same idea that's been running through this entire book: **YOU ARE AT YOUR BEST WHEN YOU ARE CONFIDENT.** Be confident in your decision to have sex—or not. If you **DEMAND RESPECT**, you will surely get it.

Splitsville

I've been dating this guy for a year and three months. Lately it seems like he's losing interest. I've talked to him about it several times, but nothing changes! I really don't want to lose him, but he just can't grasp what's wrong!

It's going to happen. There will almost definitely come a time in a relationship when one or both of you are unhappy. That's healthy and normal—otherwise, all the adults you know would be married to their high school sweethearts. And college wouldn't be half as much fun as it actually is.

Still, a breakup hardly seems healthy and normal when you're in the middle of one. Then, the whole experience is confusing, scary, and heartbreaking—whether you're the dumper or the dumpee. But, with a little preparation, you can rise above even the saddest breakup.

Here are the warning signs to look out for.

WARNING: HEARTACHE AHEAD

My boyfriend and I hardly see each other. We don't talk like we used to. Every time we're on the phone we sit there waiting for the other one to say something.

My boyfriend and I have been together a little over a year and a half. Lately it seems like all we've been doing is fighting. Will things ever get back to normal?

My boyfriend used to call me every day, compliment me, and majorly flirt with me. Now he rarely calls, never comes over to me when he sees me, and basically acts as if he doesn't know me. Why is he acting so different?

Very rarely does a breakup come out of nowhere—but suspecting trouble and confirming it are two different things. Depending on your personality, after noticing three or more of the following signs, you may want to egg his car and T.P. his house—or you may want to hide tearfully in your bedroom until graduation.

While neither of those gut reactions is wrong, they're also not the best way to handle the situation. Instead, try these effective approaches to getting to the bottom of his weird behavior.

He becomes distant, and doesn't call as much. Call *him*. And when you do, pay attention to his spoken and unspoken cues. If you're doing all the talking, don't bother asking him what's wrong. He'll probably just answer "Nothing, I'm just tired, that's all." Instead, try a more direct approach. Tell him you've noticed that he seems preoccupied, and that you think it's time to talk about where this relationship is going.

He starts flirting with other girls. Rather than storm off when he starts playfully pulling your best friend's ponytail, remain cool until you're alone together. Then call him on it. Sometimes guys really don't realize they were flirting. But if he makes a habit of it, especially when you're around, you should initiate a Talk.

He starts noticing other girls. It's one thing to mention Britney Spears's kickin' physique. It's quite another to whistle under his breath at girls he passes as you two stroll through the mall. Try a little gentle nudging—as in, "Umm, there's no need to be looking at her legs when you have me right here, thank you very much." If this doesn't break him of his uncool behavior, then you should definitely have a Talk.

His friends start dropping hints about a breakup. You can't believe everything his friends tell you—especially if they've never really warmed up to you. Breakups that started because of rumors almost always lead to regret.

He spends more time with his buddies. Give this one a fair shot. He may be trying to make it up to the guys for all the times he ditched their standing Saturday night arcade duel in favor of snuggling with you in front of HBO. But if the ratio of You Time to Them Time takes a sudden dive in their favor, request a date.

If he can't commit to a night with his girl, you might want to question his commitment, period.

He acts weird. This may sound vague. But you need to go with your instincts. If you notice a shift in his behavior toward you, it could well mean something is wrong. Does he roll his eyes and groan when you tell a funny story? Or has he broken more dates with you than you can remember, telling you that he just has "stuff to do"? If he's been consistently out of whack, trust your gut—and look out for other clues that something is up.

He doesn't pay attention to you. One day he's dropping his bookbag and lacrosse gear to give you a bear hug; the next week he barely gives you a nod as he rushes off to practice. What's up with his hot-and-cold attitude? If he's particularly stressed (like if his lacrosse team made it to the state finals), you should cut him some slack. But if there is no obvious cause for him to be so cold, tell him how you feel. If apologies and explanations don't come tumbling out of his mouth, remind yourself that you deserve to be showered with attention from a boyfriend.

He picks fights over stupid things. You mention how much you love classic soul music, and he calls you stupid. Or you giggle while telling him his new haircut makes him look like Jerry Lewis, and he snarls that you have no taste anyway. If he's picking on you—and picking fights—for no good reason, something must be bugging him. Don't let him refuse to talk about it.

He flat-out avoids you. Have you been noticing lately that every time you walk into a room, he finds an excuse to walk out? Or that whenever you call his house, his little sister tells you he's napping, or showering, or out with the dog? If he's already warned you that these next few weeks are superbusy ones for him, then ease up on your paranoia. But if something smells fishy—like the fact that he doesn't even own a dog—try to get some time with him and find out what the deal is.

He doesn't kiss you as often. For example, has he suddenly quit greeting you with a lengthy smooch when he stops by your locker? Or when he walks you home after a party, does he drop you at the door and take off, without first engaging you in a make-out moment under the porch light? Try snuggling up to him one more time. If he still treats you like a kid sister, ask him to explain.

You hear rumors that he's cheated on you. We'll say it again: Rumors should be considered fiction until proven fact. But a major rumor like this shouldn't be completely ignored. Presumably, you and your sweetie have a certain amount of trust between you, so it makes no sense to accuse him outright. If the rumor is plausible enough to bother you (like, everyone's saying he hooked up with his ex-girlfriend the weekend you and your family flew to Cancun), you could casually mention it to him. If he acts furious that anyone would make up such hurtful lies, you might decide to believe him. If he confirms the rumor and initiates a Talk, you'll be happy (in the long run, at least) to have gotten to the bottom of the story rather than blissfully ignoring it.

EIGHT REASONS HE MIGHT DUMP YOU (THAT AREN'T ABOUT YOU AT ALL)

Warning signs may prepare you for the split, but when the dump occurs, the first thing you're likely to ask is "Why?"

Sometimes it's because you simply weren't right for each other. (Vague, we know, but still true. You'll understand that excuse better when you do meet the right guy.) Other times, despite that insecure inner voice that whispers, "This is all my fault," the big dump isn't about you at all. In fact, there are many reasons why he might need to be girlfriendless right now:

1. **He's having family problems.** When your life is turned upside down at home, it can be hard to deal with other aspects of your world. Problems like illness, death, or divorce within his family might make him want to keep the rest of his life as simple as possible. And that could mean letting you go, no matter how much he cares about you. While you might want to be there to comfort him in his time of need, some people prefer to withdraw while their family crises are being worked out.

2. **He's not emotionally ready for a girlfriend.** There's a reason boys and girls don't start dating in pre-K. They aren't mature enough. And though your guy has grown up since his cut-and-

paste days, he still might not be able to handle the emotional closeness of a girlfriend-boyfriend relationship. In this case, you have to give him credit, rather than a punch in the arm, for realizing that he still has some growing up to do before he can seriously date a girl.

3 **He's really too busy.** What drew you to him was his drive and ambition: he wants to make varsity soccer as a freshman, complete high school in three years, and graduate from Princeton summa cum laude before he's twenty-one. Though his goal-oriented lifestyle is a turn-on, it might also severely limit the time and energy he has to spend on you. And this smart guy can see that, which is why he's ending things before you start to resent him and his full plate.

4 **He's brokenhearted.** Sure, he cares about you, but he might still be wounded from a previous relationship. And he knows that it isn't fair to make you live through his lapses into ex-girlfriend depression. He might need time and space to mourn his last relationship before committing fully to one with you.

5 **He's moving.** You have to respect him for trying to be noble. Sure, you could attempt a long-distance relationship, but that grows more and more difficult the more miles there are between you. And if both of you are relying on older siblings and parents for transportation, things get even trickier. Maybe he's convinced himself that you'd be better off forgetting about him now, and feeling free to date other guys once he's gone.

6 None of his guy friends have girlfriends. As much as you'd hope that if he really liked you, he'd be proud to be the only guy in his group without season tickets to the monster truck rally, it just isn't so. Peer pressure is a powerful thing, and just as your girlfriends are very important to you, his buddies—and their opinions—might rank pretty high on his priority list.

7 He's girl-crazy. This boy is all about the thrill of the chase. His feelings for you were genuine when he offered to walk you home from the end-of-school picnic, and when he admitted that holding your hand gave him the chills. He was all about treating you like his destiny—until you declared that the feelings were mutual. And now, because there are so many other girls out there he could be mooning over, he's cutting you loose. No biggie—you don't want a boyfriend with a wandering eye, anyway.

8 He's confused about his sexuality. Face it: It is completely possible that a guy might be dating a girl and suddenly realize he doesn't want to be dating *girls*. Sexuality is a confusing thing, especially when you are a teenager experimenting with the opposite sex for the first time. Your guy may not have a TV-drama moment and "come out" to you as you stroll along the beach together, but he may nevertheless be confused. And as someone who cares about him, you need to be respectful of him, his feelings—and his privacy.

REALITY CHECK

SHOULD YOU DUMP HIM?

Say your sweetie is still devoted to you, but *you're* feeling a little trapped and bored. Are you ready to cut him loose altogether? Let's think of your boyfriend as a fashion basic from your wardrobe. This quiz will help you determine whether he's in the collection for keeps, or whether he's destined for the discard pile.

1 You come home from a weekend with your dad to find your boyfriend waiting for you with flowers and Taco Bell takeout. You
   a Groan before you even get out of the car. Can't he let you have ten minutes to yourself?
   b Sigh, feeling guilty that he treats you so well.
   c Grin happily. You were hoping to see him before school on Monday.

2 You visit your cousins in another town, and go to a pool party at their neighbor's house. One of the guys there keeps grabbing your towel and playfully splashing you. It makes you feel
   a Flustered. You haven't felt this giddy since you first started dating your guy.
   b Flattered. It's like they say: As soon as you have a boyfriend, other guys want you.
   c Frustrated. You wish you weren't tied down, because then maybe you could kiss this guy.

3 Your babe is such a klutz. You used to find it cute when he'd walk into walls or trip down stairs. Now you just find it

a Scary. You don't want him getting hurt.

b Annoying. Why can't he just be normal?

c Old. He doesn't have to try to get your attention—he already has it.

4 He's coming over to watch movies tonight. To get ready, you

a Wash your face and put on leggings and a T-shirt. It's nice to feel so comfortable around him.

b Do nothing. Your philosophy is "Love me, love my Cheetos breath."

c Slick on some lip gloss. It keeps your lips soft for making out.

5 When he puts his arms around you, you

a Flinch. He's so into PDA.

b Sit there. He always does this.

c Shrug your shoulders and smile. It feels nice.

SCORING:

1. a) 1 b) 2 c) 3
2. a) 2 b) 3 c) 1
3. a) 3 b) 1 c) 2
4. a) 2 b) 1 c) 3
5. a) 1 b) 2 c) 3

(13-15) New boots

Seriously, girl, you had no business taking this quiz. If you're wondering if you should end things with your sweetie, you're just having a momentary lapse of romantic reason. It's okay to crave the attention of other guys, especially when you are as hung up on your boyfriend as you obviously are. Maintain this high level of compatibility by taking the advice given to the girls who treat their guys more like worn sweaters (below). Keep things fresh, and you'll both be happy.

(9-12) Worn sweater

Okay, so you don't get butterflies in your tummy at his very touch anymore. It happens. But you still care deeply about your boyfriend, so it's worth making an effort to keep your relationship alive. Learn to jet ski together, go out on double dates with newer couples, and try to liven up what's become a comfortable, predictable romance. If you haven't completely lost that loving feeling, you can both make an effort to keep it as fresh as a clean pair of pajamas.

(5-8) Smelly sneakers

Ditch this guy already! This relationship has run its course, and he is about as useful to you as a pair of old Reeboks. Of course, you shouldn't tell him that. But it isn't fair to your boyfriend to keep him hanging on when you find his very presence a buzz kill. It will only make both of you miserable. So tell him how you feel, but soften the blow. Tell him your early feelings of passion and lust have given way to a friendly vibe.

A CLEAN BREAK

I have a boyfriend, but I like another guy and he likes me back. I don't know how to tell my boyfriend that it is over. I'm scared. What should I do?

I have so many mixed feelings about my boyfriend. Some days I think he is wonderful, and other days I find him repulsive. I catch myself looking at other guys and wondering what I am missing. Should I break up with him?

I'm having some troubles with the guy I am in love with. One day he's all lovey-dovey, and the next he pushes me away. I talked to him about it, and he says he is confused, and that he needs time. I think he's going to break up with me, and I am really sad and scared.

Getting dumped—or dumping someone—can give you more knots in your stomach than any other stage in a relationship. If you thought you felt like barfing when you decided to ask him out, wait until you go through this. But honestly, whether you are the dumper or the dumpee, you'll feel much better once this dying relationship is behind you. To make the process as quick and painless as possible, consider these scenarios.

HE ENDS IT

What he says: "I don't want to go out with you anymore." Guys are usually pretty direct. They are also usually pretty skimpy on details.

What you should say: "Why?" There's nothing wrong with asking him for a reason. But if you are going to ask, be prepared to hear that

a He just wants to be your friend.

b You won't give him what he wants sexually.

c He wants to date another girl.

And when you hear his reason, you can righteously call him whatever name you want, but don't try to change his mind. If he's gone this far, he's not likely to hear your persuasive argument and say "Oh, you're right. I don't want to break up after all. Let's still be boyfriend-girlfriend."

How you feel: Probably pretty crappy, especially depending on what his excuse for dumping you is. You may want to cry, throw your brush against the wall, stop eating, cry some more, and not talk to anyone except your best friend for weeks. Any and all of those reactions are perfectly normal, but just try to remind yourself that you can get over this. It's nearly impossible to believe while you are going through it, but it's true: This happens to everyone at some point in their lives. And it is totally possible to have a full recovery from heartbreak. It takes time, but it will get better.

YOU END IT

What you should say: "I don't feel the same way about you that I used to." Be straight, but not cruel. You don't have to list the myriad reasons he bugs you—that would only make him feel bad. But understand that no matter how gently you break it to him, he may still think you're a witch.

Guys open up
and share their
worst breakup
experiences ever:

*"She just started
dating another
boy without telling
me."*
—Jonathon

*"She didn't let me
know face-to-face.
She wrote me a
letter and left it
for me when she
went out of town."*
—Casey

*"She told me in
front of my friends."*
—Steven

*"She just stopped
communication."*
—Drew

*"She did it over
the phone."*
—Nicolas

*"She broke up with
me on my answer-
ing machine!"*
—Mark

What he might say: "Fine, whatever." (Though if he's
the sensitive, share-your-feelings type, he might break
down and cry "Why me, why me?" In that case, treat
him gently, but don't go back on your gut reaction,
which is to end things completely.) He'll probably just
act like it's no big deal. And if he's feeling really hurt
and defensive, he may pretend you took the words out
of his mouth. So don't be shocked or insulted if he
says, "Yeah, I've been thinking the same thing. Thanks
for doing it first." Chances are he's trying to save a shred
of self-respect, the only way he knows how.

How he'll feel: About the same way you'd feel if
he'd broken up with you. So give him some room. And
though you may want to call him to see how he's taking
things, or to complain about the wicked fight your mom
started with you (after all, he's been your best friend
and confidant for months), don't. Let him get over you.

BREAKUP
DOS AND DON'TS

DO break up with him in person. Writing him a break-up note or dumping him over the phone is cowardly. It may seem like the easy way out, but it's not worth the guilt you'll feel later.

DON'T turn a private breakup into a public spectacle—whether you are the dumper or the dumpee. Keep this painful moment between the two of you. Then call all your friends once you're alone.

DO remember that he is only one of many, many guys you will date in your single-girl lifetime.

DON'T "get revenge" by hooking up with his best friend, or spreading rumors about the fact that he can't kiss, or cries at *Little House on the Prairie* reruns. Instead, get a notebook and write a list of the many reasons he was wrong for you.

DO keep your confidence up. You're fabulous! So what if it wasn't the kind of fabulous he was looking for?

DON'T become a shut-in. Go to parties, eat out, chat on the phone.

(Breakups are hard.) They inspire feelings of guilt, failure, loneli-
ness, unworthiness, and sometimes relief. But you can get through
them. Because with each relationship, **YOU LEARN** something
about yourself, about the way you relate to others, and about
what you really want from a boyfriend. All of those discoveries are
important.

   In the end, you may benefit more from a breakup than you
ever did from the relationship itself. **REALLY.**

chapter 9

Getting Over Him

My boyfriend broke up with me almost three months ago. My friends tell me I need to get over him, and I agree, but I miss him so much. What can I do?

There is no set recovery period when it comes to breakups. How can you put a time limit on a healing heart? The only thing we can guarantee is that you will recover, and your heart will heal, no matter how badly it might be hurting right now.

How long it takes you to get out of Dumpsville depends on who broke up with whom, what the excuse was, whether you saw it coming, etc. However, it's safe to say that unless your ex-boyfriend was a huge jerk all along, you'll miss him, whether you initiated the split or not.

So how can you get over the breakup and feel like your normal, happy self again? Here are a few ideas.

THE SIX-STEP "GET HIM OUT OF YOUR SYSTEM" SYSTEM

Oof. He broke things off and it felt like Cupid kicked the life out of you. Your stomach is in knots, your appetite is gone, and your eyes look permanently red-rimmed. You're convinced you will never have another boyfriend again.

But you know what? You will go on to other relationships. You might be the one breaking someone's heart next time. Or maybe—sad but true—you'll have your heart broken again. But by that time, you will have developed your own personal recovery plan, based on these steps:

Step 1: Eat—even if you're only in the mood for strawberry-banana yogurt with crunchy granola. Wasting away over love went out of style along with corsets. On the other hand, don't start bingeing on pizza to fill up the hole he left in your world. Try to keep food and love separate. But don't feel guilty about treating yourself to a bowl of Phish Food ice cream, if you really want it.

Step 2: Let it all out. Cry, scream, mope, and whimper—in the comfort of your own home, and to whichever friends and family members will listen. Haul out your thesaurus and look up every synonym for "jerk."

Step 3: Tell him how you feel. We aren't suggesting you page him on his beeper. Write him a long letter, telling him how you felt when he dumped you, how much you cared about him, how you feel post-split, and what you think of him. Then, once you've reread the letter a couple of times, walk over to a garbage can, rip the letter into tiny pieces, and throw it away.

Step 4: Appreciate yourself. Gaze at your lovely reflection in the mirror, admire the stenciled border you painted around your bedroom, review your straight-A report card, and recite your best poems aloud while you shave your legs. Paying attention to what's most wonderful about you will lift your spirits and renew your self-confidence.

Step 5: Show your ex-bozo that he doesn't know what he's missing. Apply a little cover-up to the bags under your eyes, and remember to smile and hold eye contact the next time you see him. Then, when you get home, exhausted from faking happiness for the six hours you were both on lifeguard duty at the neighborhood pool, hug your cat or dog for a little warm-and-cuddly therapy.

Step 6: Reclaim your social life. Don't avoid clubs or other favorite extracurricular activities because you feel depressed. Go out dancing with friends, talk to classmates you've never spoken with before, and make an effort to meet new people. It may be a struggle at first, but pretty soon you'll be looking forward to these activities.

A few tried-and-true recovery tactics:

"I threw out his phone number, gave him back all his stuff, and hung out with my friends."
—Seymantha

"I wrote a list of all the bad things about him and kept the list where I could see it."
—Kate

"I had a huge sleepover with my best girlfriends, ate lots of junk and had a blast, realizing that guys aren't worth the trouble."
—Tyra

"My single friends got me looking for hotties again."
—Melanie

"I kept busy with friends, other guys, working out, schoolwork, etc."
—Beth

HELP FOR GIRLS WHO'VE BANISHED THEIR BOYS TO DUMPSVILLE:

Yes, he's probably feeling a whole lot lousier than you are right now. And he might even be blaming you for tearing up his heart.

The thing is, it's also pretty likely that you're feeling down, too. That's normal. Even though you brought about the breakup, you're entitled to feel a little sad and remorseful. You've spent serious time and energy getting to know your now-ex boyfriend, and you won't be able to banish warm thoughts of him the minute you declare the relationship officially over. Memories of the amazing post-volleyball back massages he used to give you and the adorable way he licked ice cream from your fingers are sure to pop into your head when you least expect them (like during your math final).

It's okay to smile inwardly at the fond and fuzzy images, but create a full flashback, recalling also why you broke up with him. Give in to your gloom, rather than assume that your sadness means you've made a terrible mistake, and that you must get him back immediately. If you broke up with him, you had good reason. If you're feeling down because of it, try going through the above six-step recovery process. You'll feel better.

DOS AND DON'TS FOR GETTING OVER HIM

DO indulge in a pedicure, kick-boxing lessons, or an entire shelf of Danielle Steel paperbacks.

DON'T worry that you have a tragic flaw. Just because you two weren't right together, it doesn't mean that there's something wrong with you.

DO get friendly with guys. You don't have to be looking for love to appreciate male attention.

DON'T reread love notes he wrote you when things were perfect. Pack all "him" memorabilia away, to look at and laugh over in a few years.

DO spend Q.T. with your friends. Nothing can bring on temporary breakup amnesia like a wild night out with the girls.

DON'T feel silly about feeling sad. You are perfectly justified in moping around for a few weeks. Just don't make it a semester-long project.

BOYFRIEND TO BOY FRIEND

It makes sense that you'd want to be friends with your ex. After all, you've logged many phone hours getting to know everything about him. You've taught him to bake devil's food cake, he's shown you how to kick butt at Sega, and in truth, you've grown pretty attached to him—even if one or both of you no longer feels "that way" about the other. But though friendship with a former boyfriend seems like a natural progression, there's a reason that "Let's just be friends" is the most dreaded sentence in the relationship vocabulary. More often than not, the person suggesting the friendship has no intention of actually *being* friends.

WHEN IT WORKS

My boyfriend broke up with me. His excuse was "This relationship isn't going anywhere and I think we should be friends." I had no problem with that, except we aren't friends. Whenever I see him he says a quick "Hi" and then scampers off. Should I give up?

Some guys have warped ways of thinking when it comes to ex-girlfriends. For example: If he breaks up with you using the old "friends" line, and then you actually treat him like a friend, he will assume that you still like him. (You know—*like* him, like him.) It's practically inconceivable to most boys that you could get over the breakup and want nothing more than friendship from them.

In this instance, the best way to begin a friendship with your ex is to let a little air out of his overinflated ego. Flirt with other guys at school (or wherever else you see your ex, like work or summer camp). You don't have to throw yourself at his best friends, but if word gets around that you're interested in someone else, he'll come to realize you aren't pining away for him. And then he'll understand (finally!) that you really do just want to be friends.

When light dawns, his first friendly overture might be a casual "hello." After that, he'll start joking around with you, and then you two can resume the comfortable relationship you once had—minus the kissing and hand-holding.

WHEN IT DOESN'T WORK

I went out with one of my really good buddies. He told me he loved me, and then he dumped me! He wants us to be friends again, but right now it hurts to be his friend, because I still like him a lot. What should I do?

A friendship between exes can never work when one half of the former couple wants to get back together. If you still aren't over him, or he isn't over you, it will be way too painful to piece together a friendship from the remains of your romance. So what can you do if you're the one still hoping for a reunion tour? Spend plenty of time with friends and family, and without him. It's okay to temporarily avoid places you're likely to run into each other—though your heartache isn't a good enough excuse to cut earth science class just because he's in it, too. If you give yourself enough space and perspective, you may eventually find that the only feelings you have left for him are ones of friendship.

THE EX FACTOR

Building a friendship out of a relationship is only one of the many challenges you may be faced with when dealing with your ex. No matter who initiated the split, you're bound to run into your boy again and again. He still takes algebra with you, still in-line skates at the same park, and still works three storefronts down from you at the Wal-Mart shopping center.

When you do bump into each other, one of many emotions will likely come bursting forth. But don't panic. We've got plenty of tips for ways to stifle—or give in to—your feelings.

JEALOUSY

I went out with this guy for a year. We broke up, but we both still worry about each other meeting other people, and I get extremely jealous when other girls are interested in him. What's going on here?

Old habits die hard. It's perfectly natural to find yourself checking out the girls your ex pays attention to, now that he's no longer with you. While your first instinct might be to scream "Eww" at the top of your lungs when you spy some other girl slathering lotion on his back at the beach, try to refrain. He isn't your guy anymore, and whoever she is, she isn't your competition. If you must be catty (and sometimes it's hard to resist), keep your snippy comments between you and your friends.

REGRET

I was with this guy for almost a year. We were so close, we were like soul mates. I cheated on him—I guess I was curious—and he broke up with me. I begged him to take me back, but he said no, and now I don't know what to do.

If you made a mistake in the relationship—like cheating with another guy—you can't blame your ex for not wanting you back.

There are other mistakes you might have made, as well. Maybe you acted on a rumor and broke it off, only to find out he wasn't making out with your best friend at that party. Whatever the situation, if you miss him, you should let him know. Tell him you were wrong, and you're sorry. But once you state your case, no amount of cajoling, crying, or begging will make it stronger. If he no longer feels the same, the only thing you can do is learn from the experience and move on. (More on that later.)

ANGER

I went with this guy for about three months. Then I broke up with him. Afterward, his friends claimed he told them that he dumped me and that I was the B-word. What's up with that?

Everyone has the potential to be obnoxious. And ex-boyfriends are no exception. Yet it might still come as a shock when a guy behaves like a jerk toward you. Name-calling and lying about a breakup are among the most common things to do in the history of breakups. Unfortunately, it comes down to your word against his.

Still, you should call him on it. Corner your ex and let him know exactly what you think of his immature lies. Remind him that you two once cared about each other. His behavior probably stems from a bruised ego, but that's no reason for him to verbally beat you up.

(LUST)

A little while ago I messed around with an old flame. Afterward, I asked him if we'd ever be a couple again. He said he really liked me but wanted to be single for a while. I feel so used.

Why wouldn't you be attracted to your ex? After all, you've kissed him before, and he knows how to put his arms around you without hitting your ticklish spots. Plus, now that you two are broken up, many of the strains in your old relationship have melted away.

In theory, there's nothing wrong with rekindling the hot and heavy feelings you once had. But if one of you reads more into the hookup than the other does, feelings are going to be hurt.

In the future, *before* you start making out, make sure you both agree that this is just for fun, not for keeps.

(THE REBOUND)

We'll keep this tidbit short and sweet: Beware of rebound boys. Only get involved in another relationship if you can't live without *this* guy—not if you just can't live without guys.

The bottom line: You're back, baby, and better than ever. So what if all your friends have boys right now, and you're flying solo? No big deal. Love your single self, and enjoy this time alone.

The Last Word

Maybe you've read this book before you're even allowed to date. Or maybe a friend bought it for you after a bad breakup. No matter what your reasons, we hope that what you've read has helped.

Here are the things you should remember:

Liking boys is a blast. But remember not to fall for an image. And also remember that some boys are simply off limits. If you have any doubt as to whether your crush is appropriate, run it past a girlfriend. And if you feel stupid doing that—because you're crushing on *her* boyfriend—take it as a sign that things won't work out with you and him.

Catching a guy's eye is all about flaunting your natural beauty and charm. Don't look in the mirror and find fault with yourself. Instead, focus on what's fabulous and unique about you. Boys almost always think confidence and honesty are turn-ons. However, in your attempt to get his attention, don't obsess. Finding the street where he lives is good. Taking a piece of his front lawn back to your bedroom is bad. And pay attention to clues that he might be liking you back.

Catching his eye is one thing—starting a conversation is another. Flirting, like talking, is a piece of cake, especially after you've taken a little time to get your strategies in order. Phone conversations have their own set of rules, but the most important is to call with a reason. If you have nothing to say to him, you can't possibly expect a chat to go well.

Making the transition from crush to boyfriend requires one middle step: a date. You can ask him out, get friends to play Cupid, or wait for him to ask you. The choice is yours. Plus, dating itself doesn't have to mean a nighttime dinner and movie outing. You can turn any get-together, group or other-wise, into a romantic encounter.

After going out a few times and spending every free moment together, you probably want to officially become boyfriend and girlfriend. Just remember that commitment is a respon-sibility, even when you face difficulties like friends who don't like your man, or parents who disapprove of the relationship. If you think you're ready, then go for it.

Love is wonderful, but often confused with being in like or in lust. Those things are all good—it's just helpful to know the difference. And when you know it's love, you probably want to scream it from the rooftops. Just remember to keep your sense of balance. You need to balance all aspects of your life with your guy, rather than making him the focus of your world.

Kissing is fun, and anyone can learn to do it right. Just remember to breathe—and wipe away stray drool with as little fanfare as possible. Sex, on the other hand, is serious. You should never allow others to influence your decision to sleep with someone. Only you can determine how far you want to go with a guy. And you should make that decision after you've brushed up on your knowledge of STDs and pregnancy prevention, and after you've thought about all the possible outcomes of sleeping with a guy.

It's almost certain that, at some point in your life, you will be dumped. At another time, you might very well be the one doing the dumping. The most important thing to remember, no matter who initiates the split, is that nobody's feelings should be intentionally hurt, and that both of you really will go on to love again.

Getting over a split takes time, but with our six-step recovery plan, you'll be back on your feet and dry-eyed before you know it. Lean on friends, family, and others for support. And remember: You were terrific before you started going out with him, and even though you are no longer a couple, you are still just as terrific. Oh, and if you want to be friends with him again, first you need to make sure that neither of you is secretly wishing for a lovey-dovey reunion.

That's it. **THE REST IS UP TO YOU.** Now go out there and sparkle, and don't let anyone tell you you're dull. As long as you keep your interests, family, and friends in your life 24-7, you will continue to be a well-balanced, worthwhile person—and someone any guy should be happy to know.

HAVE CONFIDENCE. As long as you recognize what's so great about you, others will, too.

seventeen

Follow four high-school heroines—Kerri, Jessica, Erin
Maya—during the most exciting time of their lives. Th
love, friendship, and huge life decisions ahead. It
about to happen—just as they're *Turning Seventeen*.

Turning Seventeen #1
Any Guy You Want

Kerri makes a bet with her friends that she
will get cute, popular Matt Fowler to ask her
out—and she wins. But her plans backfire
when Matt finds out about the bet. Will
things work out for Kerri—or will she lose the
one guy she really wants, and her best
friends, too?

Turning Seventeen #2
More Than This

Jessica is already taking college courses.
She's smart. She's not the kind of girl who
cheats on her boyfriend. And she loves Alex.
Really. But Scott is totally amazing.
Now she's not sure what kind of girl she is.

SEVENTEEN BOOKS...
FOR THE TIMES OF YOUR LIFE.
Wherever books are sold.

Books created and produced by Parachute Publishing, L.L.C., distributed by HarperCollins Children's Books, a division of HarperCollins Publishers.
© 2000 PRIMEDIA Magazines, Inc., publisher of **seventeen**. Seventeen is a registered trademark of PRIMEDIA Magazines Finance Inc.